# Investigating *Can Be* Deadly

**Ron Day**

*© Copyright Ron Day, Australia 2023*

Morris Publishing Australia
http://morrispublishingaustralia.com

A catalogue record for this work is available from the National Library of Australia

i

# Investigating *Can Be* Deadly

ISBN: 978-0-6457598-3-9

The right of Ron Day to be identified as the author of this work has been asserted by him.

**All rights reserved.**



This is a work of fiction. Names, character, places, incidents, and dialogue are products of the author's imagination or are used fictionally. Any resemblance to actual people, living or dead, events, or locales is entirely coincidental.

# Contents

# Dedication

Dedicated to my lovely wife, Elaine, who supports my writing endeavours with a smile and words of praise. I also appreciate her assistance with editing, which she does with consummate skill.

I would like also to dedicate this, the third book in a series of murder mysteries, to those who delight in reading these mysteries, perhaps with a glass of wine in hand, and who try to guess the perpetrator before the climactic scene.

# Chapter One

My phone rang insistently. *It's always insistent*, I thought. *Why can't they invent a ring that is easier on the ear?*

I smiled. *Perhaps I will be told I have won the lottery.*

I grimaced. *More likely it's a scammer trying to extract some of my hard-earned cash.*

I lifted the bane of my life. 'Sean speaking.'

'*Fratello mio, buongiorno.*'

'Good morning, Marcello. What can I do for you?'

I was surprised. I rarely received phone calls from my good friend, Marcello. He was one of Adelaide's top restauranteurs. I had helped him with serious business financial problems some years ago. Now he feeds me scrumptious food when I walk into his restaurant in Norwood Parade.

He also has a niece and a nephew who can make a computer sing. They have helped me with recent enquiries, so I know I owe him.

'I need your help,' he said quickly.

'Okay, my friend,' I replied. 'How can I help?'

'Come to my little restaurant tonight and I will explain,' he boomed in his deep voice, his heavy Italian accent giving the invitation a unique and exciting quality.

'Okay, see you then,' I replied. '*Ciao*.'

'*Grazie, Ciao*,' he said and closed the call.

My mind whizzed in circles. What problem did Marcello have? His business was now running successfully so he would have no need of my auditing skills. No matter where my thoughts went, I came up with a blank.

That evening, feeling some concern, but also some excitement about where this new project would lead, I headed towards Norwood Parade, Adelaide. The evening traffic was heavy, so it took some time to negotiate the streets and find a park.

As I walked into the restaurant, a giant of a man dressed in chef's whites bore down on me. The tall chef's hat he liked to wear made him seem gigantic. He wrapped his arms around me and lifted me from the floor.

'*Fratello mio,*' he boomed. 'It has been too long. *Vieni.*'

He put me back on the floor and guided me with his big hand in the small of my back. I was herded past the customers waiting at the front counter for their pizzas to be cooked or waiting to be guided to a restaurant table.

Some people looked in surprise and others in envy as I was conducted behind the counter and through a doorway leading to the rear of the restaurant.

He led me through the huge kitchen, where we dodged frantic chefs waving kitchen utensils like weapons of war and shouting at each other, mainly in Italian, as they hurried to complete orders.

'Hi Angelo,' I called when I saw one of Marcello's sons directing the chefs. He had helped me during the Clare Valley Food and Wine event a year or two ago.

He heard me and his face broke into a wide smile. 'Hi, Sean,' he called. 'Helping Dad again?'

I waved as Marcello gave my back another push towards a rear door. He grabbed a bottle of wine and two glasses from a counter as we walked.

We moved through the door into a small private dining area with just one set table. I was no stranger to this private space where I had enjoyed some of the most flavoursome Italian food of my life.

Marcello opened the bottle and poured us each a glass. I swirled the wine around my glass to release the esters and sniffed deeply. The aromas tickled my nose delightfully.

I took a sip and smiled my appreciation. '*Molto buon vino*,' I said in my limited Italian.

Marcello smiled at my attempt to speak his language.

'*Fratello mio.* I have a problem I think you can solve.'

I looked at him closely.

'My cousin Emilio runs a winery.'

*Ah ha,* I thought. *This sounds promising.*

'He has been losing lots of money and doesn't know where it has gone. I told him you can help him find it. His son is also missing. You might also be able to help find him.'

'I would love to help Emilio. Where is his winery?' I asked, my interest piqued.

'Queensland, in the Granite Belt,' he answered.

'Queensland? That's a long way from here,' I replied, surprised.

'He will fly you there. Here is your ticket for next Friday.'

He reached into a pocket and handed me an airline ticket.

I gasped. 'You have accepted for me?'

'*Naturalmente.* I know you will like the challenge.'

I took a deep breath and let the air escape slowly. I needed a moment to get over the shock caused by discovering my life was suddenly being taken in a new direction.

'We need to eat. *Scusi.*' Marcello rose and walked to the door. I saw him wave to his son. He spoke to him in rapid Italian and then returned to the table.

'Let us eat, then I will answer questions.'

I was still in shock but slowly beginning to look forward to this new challenge.

'Thank you, Marcello. I have lots of questions,' I said.

A stream of delicious food soon arrived at our table, beginning with antipasto. We began eating. I savoured every bite of the tasty food.

Slowly the story unfolded. Emilio's winery was in the Ballandean area near Stanthorpe in the southern part of Queensland's Granite Belt. He had noticed that substantial amounts of money were disappearing from the winery's accounts. Emilio's son, Antonio, disappeared around the time the last amount was taken out.

'Emilio says he is a good boy and is becoming an exceptionally good winemaker, but just before he disappeared, he had withdrawn from the family. He seemed worried about something but wouldn't talk about it,' said Marcello. 'Emilio thinks he might have run away from home, but he can't think of a reason why.'

I began assembling the problems in my mind and mentally listing potential solutions.

'You are good at poking your nose into other people's business and solving problems,' said Marcello with a comforting smile. 'Emilio needs you.'

'I will do my best,' I replied.

'I know you will,' said Marcello. "Emilio says bring warm clothes. The mountains are cold at this time of year.'

# Chapter Two

I always enjoy flying. I love to watch other passengers and note their interactions. Some people talk to their neighbours, some read, others pretend to sleep. I watched one woman trying to get comfortable next to a very large person who really needed a seat and a half.

She squirmed uncomfortably for some time before calling over a hostess. I could hear her complaining. Eventually, after a heated discussion, she was moved to a spare seat further down the plane.

The plane landed smoothly at the Brisbane airport. I climbed from my seat to stand in a crowded aisle. Many of us reached up to open overhead lockers so we could retrieve our hand luggage. After some time, the queue finally moved towards the plane door.

A hostie farewelled me as I stepped through the door and joined the other passengers walking along the aerial tunnel into the Arrivals Lounge.

Near the doorway to the baggage claim area, a well-dressed man stood holding a large card to his chest. His dark hair and swarthy complexion spoke volumes of his Italian ancestry. The frown on his face suggested this was not something he did regularly.

"Sean O'Connor" was written on the card in large letters.

I walked up to him and said, 'I'm Sean. You must be Emilio.'

A smile broke across his face, replacing the worried look of a moment ago.

He took my hand in his. 'Welcome to Queensland. Marcello tells me you are good at helping people with money problems,' he gushed.

'Thank you for the plane ticket,' I said. 'I will do whatever I can to help you.'

'Marcello says you worked magic when he had money problems. I hope you can help me too with my missing money. You might also be able to help find my son. We think he has run away but we are not sure.'

'Sorry to hear about your son. Let's talk about those problems later,' I suggested as we walked towards the baggage collection area. 'Tell me about your winery.'

'What do you know about wineries?' he asked, his head turned towards me to gauge my response.

I smiled. 'I have worked closely with a number of wineries in South Australia, and I grow wine grapes in the Clare Valley in my spare time,' I replied.

Emilio sighed with relief, 'Then Marcello has chosen the right person.'

I collected my luggage from the carousel, and we walked to the carpark. Emilio stored my luggage in the car boot, and we began our three-hour journey to the Granite Belt.

As we drove, I discovered that commercial wine grape growing began quite recently in the Granite Belt. Many workers, including a sizeable number of Italians and Chinese had worked in the Stanthorpe tin mines until they closed in the 1890's. Later some of the miners turned to growing fruit and table grapes. Eventually, many turned to wine grapes, which they processed locally.

Emilio gave me a potted history of his family's time in the Granite Belt then talked about the grapes they grow and the wines they make. It was the story of a profitable winery. Nothing suggested a reason for losing lots of money or losing a son.

I changed the topic. 'Emilio, I would like to stay somewhere away from your vineyard. I want to appear as a casual visitor to the area. That way it will be easier for me to investigate.'

Emilio smiled. 'Marcello said you would want that, so I have booked a place in your name. I'll take you there when we reach Ballandean. I'll lend you a vehicle.'

'Thank you, Emilio, but no. I don't want to drive a vehicle that other people will recognise. I would like you to take me to a vehicle hire place in Stanthorpe. I will hire my own wheels.'

'Okay,' he replied. 'I am beginning to see you have done this before.'

'Once or twice,' I replied with a smile.

Eventually, we pulled up in front of a vehicle hire business and I walked in.

I looked at several cars in the yard then noticed a motorbike standing to one side. I smiled. *Not a Bike like mine but it will do.*

Before long, I walked out to the bike with loan helmets and gloves in my hands. I climbed into the saddle and rode out to sit behind Emilio's car.

'Let's go,' I shouted over the engine noise, waving my gloved hand to indicate I was ready.

Emilio's surprised face stared at me for a moment then he turned and started his car. I followed him as we travelled south towards Ballandean. We reached the centre of the town then took several side roads. Before long he pulled up in front of three attractive buildings. I noticed the large sign announcing they were the Cabernet Cabins.

Emilio pointed. 'The front one is for you.'

He produced keys and took me in. I was pleased by the comfort and space, and the bottle of Cabernet wine from a local winery waiting to be opened on the dining room table. I explored, while Emilio brought my luggage from his car.

'This is amazing,' I said. 'Thank you for booking this place for me. I will be extremely comfortable.'

Emilio turned to leave.

'I will come to see you in the morning,' I said.

'I will look forward to that,' he said as he turned and walked back to his car.

# Chapter Three

The next morning, I was up early. After a shower and some breakfast, I grabbed a district winery map from the cabin and read the directions to Emilio's Top of the Range Winery. I mounted the motorbike and set off.

When I arrived, I stared in awe at the winery's main building. It was huge. As I walked in, I was amazed by the rich Italian treatment of the rooms I walked through. Strong colours and textures, together with lots of wood, gave an immediate sense of permanency and quality. In one room, huge timber wine barrels told the visitors they were in a winery. The family members I met were open, friendly, and cooperative. I immediately felt at home.

'Would you like something to eat,' asked a well-dressed mature woman, obviously of Italian heritage. Her broad smile told me she was practiced at feeding visitors.

'No, Mia,' said Emilio walking into the room. 'Sean and I have things to do. We will eat later, *grazie.*'

He turned to me. 'Can you please come with me?'

He led me into his study. A slim, young, blonde woman in a smart black dress was sitting at the computer, receipts and invoices spread around her.

'What do you need to see first?' asked Emilio after introducing me to his accountant.

'Can you log me into your bank accounts?' I asked.

He looked at me. 'Jane comes in once a week to do the accounting. She is a better person to show you.'

I took a seat next to Jane. I grabbed a pen and a sheet of paper.

'How many bank accounts are there,' I asked.

'One,' she answered.

'Only one?' I asked in absolute amazement.

She nodded.

'Can you show me this one on the screen, please.'

I scanned the recent income and withdrawals lists. Several large withdrawals showed substantial amounts. My quick examination showed quite a few amounts varying between $7,000 and $19,000. The most recent of these large withdrawals was for $10,000.

'Can you say who withdrew these amounts and what they were for?' I asked Jane.

'I believe the chief winemaker withdrew most of those large amounts. I was told he needed to buy more barrels and pumps,' she answered.

'He withdraws cash?' I asked. 'That is unusual.'

Jane shrugged. 'He prefers to work that way. He has always produced invoices that match.

'Do you have any paperwork for those amounts?'

'That paperwork is stored in a folder in the winery,' she explained. 'The kitchen staff keep their expenses in another folder. I collect them monthly to check against the bank account. I am due to collect them this week.'

'Can we get those folders here quickly?' I asked Emilio.

He lifted a phone and called the winery office. When the call was answered, he asked for the folder to be brought to his office immediately. Within minutes a teenage lad came to the door and handed the folder to Emilio. He passed it to me.

He called the kitchen and asked the same question. A second folder was delivered a few moments later.

I went through the winery folder looking for paperwork for large purchases that might match the large amounts I had seen as withdrawals.

There was none.

Then it clicked. 'How often do you change the password on this account?' I asked.

'Password?' asked Emilio. 'I don't think we ever do.' He looked at Jane. 'Do you know?'

She shook her head.

'Where is your chief winemaker now?' I asked.

Emilio's face sagged. 'I had to let him go recently. He was making too many mistakes. His mind seemed to be far away much of the time, and he spent far too much time on his phone. His lack of attention led to us losing two tanks of wine. A huge financial loss for us.'

'Let him go?' I asked. 'Do you mean you sacked him?'

'Yes,' he said. 'Are you suggesting he took the money?'

'I am saying it is a distinct possibility, and I believe he may take more money if you don't change the password immediately,' I said firmly.

Jane returned to the bank account on her screen, asking Emilio for a new password. He supplied one and Jane made the change. I made a note of the password and handed the sheet to Jane to lock away.

'Emilio,' I said. 'I suggest all ordering on this account be done by Jane in the future. No one else should be able to operate on this account. She might need to work more days a week. Is that a problem?'

'Not at all,' replied Emilio. 'She can work as many days a week as we need.'

He turned to Jane. 'Are you able to work more than one day?' he asked.

'I can work three if that is acceptable,' she replied with a smile.

'Will that work, Sean?' he asked me.

'I think that would be much more useful,' I replied. 'Emilio, it is important that all paperwork is kept in this office.'

He agreed, then remembered. 'We will need to let the kitchen staff buy the food supplies they need for the large amount of catering they do.'

'Fine,' I answered. 'I suggest you have a separate account and card for catering.'

'If you suggest that then we should do it,' he answered.

'Let Jane create a special account for them to use,' I suggested. 'All the money they take from catering can be banked into that account. Kitchen staff can then use that money to fund their purchases.'

'That's a good idea,' said Emilio. 'My wife, Mia, oversees the kitchen. She will be pleased to operate her finances independently. She has often complained about not having full control of that money.'

'Good,' I said. 'Can you take care of that please, Jane?'

She nodded.

I continued addressing Jane, 'I would like you to print a copy of the bank statement. On that copy, mark off all the expenses you can find in these two folders. Also mark all moneys that have been paid in wages, tax, bank fees and vehicle registrations and insurances. It will be a long and tedious task, but it will tell us exactly how much money has disappeared and can't be accounted for.'

I turned to Emilio. 'We need to know how much money has been stolen. At some stage we will have to prove how much has been taken.'

'Do you know exactly what must be done, Jane?' I asked.

She nodded confidently. 'Of course. I do that every month.'

I turned to Emilio. 'Now can we take a look in your son's bedroom?'

We walked from the winery into the neighbouring house. Emilio led me through the rooms to Antonio's bedroom.

I walked around the room to get a feel for Antonio's private life. Nothing immediately suggested a reason for his disappearance. Then I noticed a laptop on his bedroom desk. I opened it and tried to log on. It needed a password.

'Do you have any idea what Antonio's password for his laptop might be?' I asked Emilio.

He shook his head. 'Not the faintest.'

I looked at him thoughtfully. 'Marcello has a niece and nephew who can make computers sing,' I said. 'We need them to open this computer to find out what has been happening lately in his life. Do I have your permission to call on them?'

'Of course,' he replied. 'If you say we need them, I trust you, so go ahead. I will pay for their plane fares, and we can accommodate them here.'

I opened my phone and dialled.

'*Pronto,*' was the quick reply.

'Marcello, it is me, Sean. We need your clever niece and nephew up here to help us with computer problems. Emilio says they can stay in his house.'

'*Fratello mio,*' his loud voice boomed from the phone speaker. 'Have you found where Emilio's boy and money have gone?'

'We have no idea yet where Antonio might be, but we are beginning to solve the money problem,' I answered. 'We think some of it might have been stolen, but we have more investigations to carry out before we know what really happened. What about your niece and nephew?'

'Alonzo is busy on another job for me, but Maria can come. I will arrange a flight and send you the time to collect her from the airport.'

'Excellent, thank you.'

'*Fratello mio,* for you anything. *Ciao*,' he said and closed the call.

I turned to Emilio. 'Marcello will send up his niece, Maria. Her brother is busy on another job. Can I borrow a vehicle to collect her from the airport tomorrow?'

'Of course,' he said with a smile. 'When will she arrive?'

'Marcello will let me know when he makes the flight booking.'

He nodded. 'Time to eat,' he said.

We walked back to the winery and took a table. Soon delicious food and glasses of wine were served by smiling family members. I noticed many winery visitors sitting at other tables. They were laughing and chatting freely. This was obviously a favourite place to visit.

My phone pinged to announce a message. I opened my message folder.

'Maria will arrive around lunchtime tomorrow. I'll need a vehicle in the morning around 8.30,' I told Emilio.

He nodded as he directed another forkful of pasta to his mouth.

# Chapter Four

The next morning, I collected a car from the winery and set off for Brisbane. As I drove, my mind revolved around yesterday's discoveries, and I began forming a list of questions in my mind that needed answers. My mind then shifted to Antonio's laptop. *What will we uncover when Maria opens it?* I wondered.

Her flight was on time. I stood watching the passengers coming through the Arrivals door. I saw her a moment before she spotted me. Her slim body was dressed in a smart blue outfit, and she was wearing heels. Her long black hair flowed engagingly around her shoulders as she walked. I enjoyed seeing her again. It had been some time.

When she saw me, her face lit up with a wide smile. We had worked together on several previous cases, and we combined our skills well. She has a sharp mind and sees links quickly.

As she approached, I opened my arms. She walked straight into a friendly hug.

'Thank you for coming,' I said with deep sincerity.

'Uncle Marcello said I was to help you as much as I can,' she replied. 'I just hope I can do enough without Alonzo here to help.'

'I'm sure we will manage without him,' I said with a smile. 'You are a very skilled young lady. Let's grab your baggage and hit the road. We have a three-hour journey ahead of us.'

'By the way,' I added as an afterthought. 'Have you had some lunch? If not, we can grab a bite along the way.'

'A sandwich would be great,' she replied.

We collected her bag from the circulating belt and headed out to the car. We were soon on our way. As we drove, I filled Maria in with as much of the problem as I could at that time.

'So, you think Antonio's laptop may hold important answers?' she asked.

'Exactly,' I replied. 'We are depending on you to get into that laptop without a password.'

'That is easy,' she answered. 'Microsoft has provided ways to do that.'

'Good old Microsoft,' I commented. 'I wouldn't know how to do that.'

'Would you like me to teach you?'

'Yes, please.'

The traffic was light, and we made good time back to the Granite Belt. Maria was as amazed as I had been to see the huge granite boulders that give the area its name.

When we arrived at the winery, I introduced Maria to Emilio and his wife. Mia showed her to a spare bedroom. She soon came out ready to start work.

Emilio and I showed her to Antonio's room, and she rushed straight to the laptop.

We watched in absolute amazement as she entered a few keystrokes and opened the system. Her fingers danced across the keyboard like lightning as she began exploring Antonio's electronic world.

'He has a girlfriend called Bella,' she said after some exploring, 'and they have been communicating through Facebook Messenger.'

'What's that?' asked Antonio's father.

I could see by his expression that he was totally lost in the modern computer world.

'It's one of the Social Media platforms where friends can share their thoughts and deeds,' she explained.

'Oh!'

'I hope her name is not "Bella Donna",' I said with a grin.

Maria looked at me with a frown on her face that said, *Don't go there.*

I looked at her in surprise. She immediately knew what I meant. She was one smart young lady.

'What is wrong with "Beautiful Woman" as her name?' asked Emilio. He obviously had not recognised the *"double-entendre"*.

'Nothing, Emilio,' I said. 'It was just a bad joke.'

'Sorry,' I said to Maria.

Her frown turned to a smile before she returned to the laptop screen. She worked back through the earlier communications between these two youngsters then returned to the latest messages.

'There is something fishy about the last messages from Bella,' she said.

We craned forward to look at the screen over her shoulders.

'What do you see?' I asked.

'The tone has changed. Her use of language is different from the earlier messages. I think these last messages were written by someone else.'

'Please explain,' I asked.

'The earlier messages are all lovey dovey just as you would expect from teenage sweethearts, and they include modern jargon used by the young. Suddenly the tone changes. It becomes more formal. She says she needs money, lots of it and asks Antonio to bring it to her. She asks for $10,000 in a cash cheque. She promises she will reward him with many kisses.'

My eyes lit up. I remembered that the last large withdrawal from the winery account was for $10,000.

Emilio was stunned. It was such a brazen request.

'I can't believe my son would be so gullible as to believe that,' said Emilio. His voice choked.

'Love is blind,' I said.

'What is the date on that message?' I asked Maria.

'Eight days ago,' she replied quickly.

'Looks as if this was the reason Antonio was withdrawn,' I said.

'There is more,' said Maria.

We look at her closely.

'What else?' I asked.

'The last message suggested he meet her late at night in two days' time at the High School bus stop near Tin Town Fine Dining.'

'So, he left here of his own volition,' said Emilio. 'We know where he went, but where is he now? That was five days ago. The other question I have … is he the one who has been taking all the money from the accounts? I hate to think he would deceive me. No, it can't be. How could I have such a thought?' He cringed, wrapped in his own doubt and misery. Emilio's face went grey. He seemed suddenly to age.

'It is possible,' I said. 'Remember the last large withdrawal from that account was $10,000. We can't blame him,' I said positively, 'until we have clear evidence. My money is on the sacked winemaker.'

'I suppose so,' said Emilio, obviously not ready to be convinced.

I turned to Jane who had followed us into Antonio's bedroom, 'Jane, can you please bring us a copy of your printout of all the outward transaction from the account for the last thirty days?'

She nodded and left the room.

'Time to investigate,' I said looking at the others. 'Question 1. Who is Bella?'

'I've never met her,' said Emilio. 'I have no idea.'

I passed the buck back to the only person who could help us answer that question. 'Over to you, Maria. You are the chief investigator on our team.'

Maria rose from her chair. 'She doesn't show her last name on her Facebook account. I need my laptop,' she explained. 'It has special software on it that I need to use. I'll get it from my bedroom,' she said as she dashed out the door.

She returned quickly, setting up her laptop next to Antonio's.

'The first place I'll look is in school records.'

'You can do that?' I questioned in surprise.

'Best place to start,' she answered as her fingers flashed over the keyboard.

I peered at the screen over her shoulder as lists of student's names rolled down the screen.

'I don't know how you did that,' I said completely in awe.

She ignored me.

Before long she said, 'Found her. Bella Marshall. Anyone know the Marshall family?' she asked. 'If not, I'll look up the Council Ratepayers list.'

Jane returned from her office with her report just in time to hear the question.

'Isn't Marshall the name of the guy who runs Tin Town Fine Dining?' she asked.

'Yes,' answered Emilio. 'I've had a run in with him. I don't trust him an inch.'

'Why is that?' I asked.

'He wanted to buy some of my wine at half price, promising some advertising,' replied Emilio. 'I told him we didn't need his advertising, that we already have a solid customer base. He wasn't happy about that but refused to pay full price, so I told him to get lost. He became angry and shouted that I would be very sorry. "Watch your son", he threatened.'

Maria and I looked at him, absorbing the implications of what he had just said.

'What happened then?' I asked.

'He slammed the phone down.'

Maria turned back to her laptop and tapped to open the Tin Town Fine Dining web page. Before long she found the name of the owner and it was indeed John Marshall.

'Bingo,' I said. 'We have a match.'

'Not quite yet. Let's see if he has a daughter called Bella,' said Maria.

*She's nothing if not thorough*, I thought. *Good quality in a researcher.*

The keyboard tapping continued. Before long, Maria had established that John and Betty Marshall have a daughter called Bella who is 17 years of age. Just the right age to have a boyfriend of 18 years called Antonio Angelica.

'Finally, we are getting somewhere.' I sighed with relief. At least some of the questions in my mind were finding answers.

I took the report from Jane and scanned down the columns. When I found the amount for ten thousand dollars, I checked the date.

'Ten thousand dollars was withdrawn the day Antonio disappeared,' I said.

Emilio's face fell. 'How could he do that?' he said then fell silent. I could see by his expression that his mind had dropped into a dark place.

# Chapter Five

The next morning, I decided it was time to begin laying a false trail. I wanted it believed that I was just a visitor to the area and a business auditor, not a private investigator. I called Maria to see whether she wanted to join me on this trip.

'No thank you, Sean,' she answered. 'I will spend my time investigating the leads we have just begun to unravel.'

I took the map I had found in the cabin that showed directions to the wineries. I studied it for a while and planned my day, then chose my first stop.

I slowed my bike as I drove through the gateway of my first winery. I came to a halt in the car park for the wine tasting area of Harmony Winery. The tropical sun warmed my soul as I doffed my helmet and stripped off my leather jacket. *It's a grand day*, my inner Dublin voice told me.

I opened the door and stepped in, sweeping my eyes around the room. A long, polished timber bench and stools awaited wine tasters.

'Good morning,' said a melodious voice from behind the bar.

'Top o' the mornin to you too,' I replied and smiled politely at the attractive young woman.

She smiled at my Irish accent. 'My mother came from Cork.' Her voice inflected the word Cork.

'I love the way you have learned the Cork accent.'

'What do you mean?' she asked, a puzzled look on her face.

'Cork people often make the last part of the word or sentence go up as if asking a question.'

She thought about that for a moment. 'What wine would you like to sample?' she asked making her voice go up when she said 'sample'.

'You've got it,' I smiled, and she laughed with me as we enjoyed our little joke.

'Let me see your wine list before I choose,' I replied as I strode across to where she was standing.

She handed me a list and I spent a few moments running my eye down it.

'Quite a selection,' I commented. 'Which would be your choice of the white wines?'

'My favourite is the Wild Child Viognier,' she offered.

'Named after you I presume,' I quipped. 'I'd like to sample that one.'

She smiled politely at my joke as she selected a bottle from a wine refrigerator, unscrewed the Stelvin cap and poured a sample into a glass.

I rotated the glass and sniffed to test the bouquet, then sampled a small mouthful, letting it run around my mouth while I tested the balance of fruit and acid.

She watched me with a growing appreciation of my wine tasting skill.

'Do you work in the wine industry?' she asked.

'You could say that,' I replied, 'I audit wineries and have worked with some great winemakers.'

Her mouth made a large 'O' shape.

At that moment, an older gentleman entered from a door behind the counter. He wore a long white coat to protect his clothes. He saw me and asked, 'Is Karen looking after you, Sir?'

'She's doing a grand job,' I replied with a smile.

'This man works in wineries,' she offered. 'He audits wineries.'

'What wineries have you audited?' he asked. His tone reflected his genuine interest.

'My work has been mostly in South Australian wineries,' I answered. 'I've come to Queensland for a holiday and thought I would like to compare the wines you make with their southern cousins. You may know some of these wineries.' I listed some I had worked with in recent years.

'Wasn't there a murder in one of those Clare Valley wineries recently?' he asked.

'You've heard of that?' I asked with some surprise.

He nodded.

'I helped identify the murderer in that one.'

'You did?

I nodded.

He looked at me closely. 'Any chance you'd like to audit this winery while you are here?'

'You haven't had any murders lately, have you?' I asked with a giveaway smile.

'None that I'm aware of,' he answered with a grin. 'Do I have to organise one before you work for me?'

'Of course not,' I answered. 'It's a relief knowing I won't find a body behind a wine vat as I audit your business.'

We both laughed. Karen looked at the two of us in wonder, then shook her head.

I thought for a moment then said, 'Okay. I have some other things to do first, but I see no reason to hurry home. I'll do your audit before I leave. By the way, my name is Sean O'Connor.'

'I'm Ted MacGregor. Pleased to have you on board.'

I handed him one of my business cards and he shared his phone number with me, then he returned through the door.

Karen continued with her introduction to their wines. Then she grabbed a wine list and turned it over. 'Here are some places you might like to visit while you are here,' she said as she began writing directions.

I was amazed at her helpfulness. She obviously loved this part of the world. As she wrote, she talked about the places she was recommending.

I thanked her profusely when she handed me the list.

'I'll make it my business to visit as many of these as possible.'

'You may not want to visit them all,' she said, 'but I love this part of the world and I want to share it with others as much as I can.'

She looked up at me from her writing. 'By the way, the Australian Small Winemakers' Show is on in Stanthorpe for a week beginning October 15th. It will give you a chance to taste wine from most of the wineries in this area as well as other states. You shouldn't miss it.'

I looked up the date on my phone. 'That's only a fortnight away. Will you be there?'

'You bet. We normally take several awards at that show.'

As I walked towards the door, I smiled and said, 'I'll see you there.'

I looked forward to finishing my investigations for Emilio and coming back to carry out an audit for these people.

# Chapter Six

I decided to visit Tin Town Fine Dining in Stanthorpe but take in some of the other places north of Ballandean on Karen's list on the way. I found that the Ballandean area was mainly wine grape growing but as I travelled north towards Stanthorpe, I saw that many other fruits were grown.

I called in to a fruit juice factory where I found bottled juices from many fruits. I tasted several and made a selection to take back to my cabin home. Not far away, I found a fruit and vegetable stall where I bought some fruit for my breakfast and stored my purchases in one of my pannier bags along with the fruit juices.

I looked on my map and located Tin Town Fine Dining. Before long, I found the building and rode my bike into the car park. As I entered the front door, a tall, sharp-eyed and well-dressed man took a long look at me with dark and penetrating eyes. I guessed he was the owner.

He walked towards me briskly. 'You're not a bikie, are you? I heard what sounded like a motorbike coming into the carpark.'

'No,' I said, 'I'm no bikie. I'm just a visitor to your part of the world who likes to ride a bike.'

I stripped off my leather jacket. 'See. No tats. No club colours.'

I turned around in a circle. 'I'm as clean as a whistle.'

He stared at me suspiciously. 'Where are you from?'

'South Australia,' I said shortly.

'What's your normal job?' he asked.

I studied him curiously. *Antonio's potential father-in-law seems a hard case,* I thought. *Why is he so inquisitive?* I decided to play his game for a while. Thinking that I might learn more about him.

'I'm a computer analyst and a certified auditor. I audit wineries. I normally work in wineries in South Australia, but I've been asked to audit some in this area,' I said firmly. 'Here is my card in case other wineries need auditing.'

I handed him several business cards from my pocket.

'Good,' he said. His tone softened a little as he read the top card. 'I'm sure some of them can do with expert help. Where are you staying?' he asked.

'In one of the Cabernet Cabins in Ballandean,' I answered.

He adopted a friendlier tone. 'I've always liked those buildings. Which one are you in?'

*This conversation is getting too personal,* I thought. *What's he up to? I had better be careful. He may be connected to the theft of Emilio's money or Antonio's disappearance.*

32

I decided to misdirect him. 'The back one.'

'Which wineries will you audit?' He was digging deep, but I decided to play along.

'First, I will work with Harmony Winery. I'm hoping they will spread the word amongst the others.'

'That's a good winery. They make some excellent wines. I am sure it will be an easy auditing job for you. I don't suppose Top of the Range Winery has approached you?'

'No, but they are on my winery list to visit.'

*I dodged his question, neatly,* I thought. *But why would he mention Emilio's winery? Was it because he had a run in with Emilio?*

Then I decided that was enough of his questions. 'Do you think I could see a menu?' I asked.

He remembered his real role. "Yes, of course. Sit at Table 6 and I'll bring one over.'

'Thank you,' I said and moved to the table.

Quickly, he arrived, bringing a menu with him and a friendlier manner. 'I can recommend the pastas,' he said. 'The chicken dishes are also popular.'

I browsed the menu and made my choice. The Spaghetti Bolognese resonated with my taste buds.

'And a wine to accompany that?' he asked.

'Just a glass of red,' I answered. 'I'm riding so I need to be careful. What do you recommend?'

'I suggest the Harmony Shiraz,' he offered. 'It is a lovely drop, and seeing you will be working there, you'll have the chance to enjoy it more.'

I smiled. It was my turn. 'Do you live on the premises?' I asked.

He looked me closely. 'Yes, my family and I live here. Why does that interest you?'

'Like you, I am interested in the people I meet,' I said smoothly.

He walked away quickly to relay my order to the kitchen and, I guessed, to avoid more questions from me. *He doesn't like the taste of his own medicine*, I thought.

The tasty Spag. Bol. and the smooth wine arrived, but my inquisitive restaurant owner had no more questions. He found bookwork to do behind the counter.

While I ate, I let my mind revolve around the issues we had so far uncovered and the problems still needing our close attention.

*Who would interfere with Bella's Messenger account and write notes to Antonio? I wondered. Surely the most likely person would be her mother. But why? Perhaps the message was intended to have him come to meet Bella. But why the money? This place looks like it is doing well. What am I missing? I need to discuss this with Maria. She is perceptive and may see links that I'm missing.*

I finished my meal, thanked my host for the delicious food and left the building.

I mounted my bike and headed for the carpark entrance. As I turned through the gateway to enter the road, I glanced back. I caught a quick glimpse of the restaurant owner's face through a window, his eyes following me. When he saw me looking, his head quickly darted away.

*Very inquisitive fellow*, I thought. *For some reason he is suspicious of me. I must keep an eye on him.*

# Chapter Seven

Back at the winery, I sought Maria and found her in Jane's office with her nose in her laptop, still hunting for clues. She impressed me with her attention to detail and unfailing energy for researching.

'I need to discuss a few things with you,' I said. 'Can you leave your computer for a while?'

'Glad to,' she answered with a smile. She rose from her chair and walked to the office door.

I loved her smile, and I loved the way she could see into the depths of whatever we were investigating quickly.

We found a table outside in the shade of a large Morton Bay Fig tree.

'What did you find out?' she asked.

'Lots, but much of it just leads to more questions.'

'Such as,' she prompted.

'Okay,' I said, 'Here we go. The first thing is I have a winery auditing job after we have solved Emilio's problems. That gives me some cover. The second is that I met John Marshall and had lunch in his restaurant. He is the most inquisitive person I have ever met. I think he suspects me, but of what, I have no idea.'

'Do you think he has something to hide?' asked Maria.

'Possibly. Almost his first question was, have I had any contact with this winery. I denied it of course. Then I began thinking about who might have interfered with Bella's Messenger conversation with Antonio. It seems to me the most likely person is her mother. Perhaps she wants to break up the friendship between these teenagers, but why?'

'That's obvious,' replied Maria quickly. 'If she made the entries in Messenger, she probably doesn't want her daughter marrying an Italian.'

I looked at her closely. 'Do you think she could be racist?'

'It is very possible. I have felt that racism myself. I know what it feels like,' she said with conviction.

I reached my hand to hold hers. 'I'm sorry. I had no idea. You are such a bright, intelligent, and beautiful young woman that no-one in their right mind would want to even think of racist comments to make about you.'

Maria placed her other hand on top of mine. 'You are colour blind and race blind. I don't think you would ever criticise another because of race, creed, or colour. That is one of the reasons I like you so much.'

I looked at her in surprise. 'Those things don't matter,' I replied. 'The only important thing is how a person acts towards others. Our differences are attitudinal and behavioural. My mother used to say, "Always do unto others as you would have them do unto you."'

Maria gave my hand a big squeeze. 'Exactly,' she said. 'Your mother was a wonderful person.'

I wanted to give her a big kiss, but this was not the moment. I blew her an air kiss instead. She smiled and reciprocated.

'Okay,' I said, breaking the moment. 'Why would a racist want Antonio to come alone to Stanthorpe?'

'To beat him up, to frighten him away from her daughter, to steal his money, to abduct him, to murder him. The list goes on,' said Maria.

'If you are right, she would need some help to do those things. Who could that be?'

'Maybe her husband. You said he was being inquisitive. Perhaps he suspects you of being an investigator,' she suggested.

'Okay,' I concluded. 'We don't have conclusive proof of any of that yet. We just have to keep digging. Tomorrow I'll visit some more wineries and ask some probing questions.'

'What would you like me to do?' she asked.

'We don't know anything yet about the sacked winemaker, Shane Mason. I would like you to see if you can find information about him. We need to know where he is and what he is doing.'

'I'll find out as much about him as I can tomorrow. I'll get his address from Emilio,' she said, 'but now I think we should let Emilio know what we have discovered so far.'

'Good thinking. You are right. We need to keep him in the loop,' I answered.

We left the table and went looking for our host.

We found him in his favourite place, the vineyard. He was striding between the rows of grapevines. He wore a large-brimmed straw hat, long-sleeved shirt, and jeans. He hummed to himself as he walked along the rows of grapevines with a pair of secateurs in his hand. I could see that a machine pruner had been along these rows recently, cutting the vines back close to the trellis. He was snipping a few canes that needed fine tuning.

He heard us talking as we walked and turned with a smile. 'How are my detectives today?' he asked.

'Still detecting,' I said. 'We are slowly making progress, but it will take some time.'

'I hope you find Antonio soon,' he said. 'We are worried about his safety. Also, we are submitting some of his wine to the Australian Small Winemakers' Show, and he needs to be there if he wins an award as I think he will.'

'That's only two weeks away,' I said, 'so the pressure is on us to locate him quickly.'

'Can you do it?' asked Emilio.

'We think we know why he disappeared, and who had a hand in making him disappear, so we are reasonably confident of getting him back on time,' I replied.

Emilio smiled his first smile for several days. 'Let's go back to the winery,' he said. 'We'll have some dinner, and you can tell me all about it.'

# Chapter Eight

I began by telling Emilio about my visit to Harmony Winery.

'They are good winemakers over there,' he said. 'Every year they win awards at the Australian Small Winemakers Show. So, they want you to audit their business? Good for you. Perhaps you should do this one too?'

'I will,' I replied. 'But for you, the extra service is free.'

'Not at all,' he said strongly. 'We pay full dollar for everything we need.'

'We'll argue about that another time,' I answered, 'Now let me tell you about my visit to Tin Town Fine Dining.'

He pricked up his ears, 'Tell me quickly.'

I related the story I had already told Maria and mentioned our thoughts about Betty Marshall.

'She is definitely one to watch,' he said, 'but you be careful. We don't want you disappearing too. Her father is one to watch too. He is devious. As I explained earlier, I don't trust him an inch. What are your next steps?' he asked looking first at me and then at Maria. He was listening intently.

'I'm visiting some more wineries. I'll be poking my nose into their businesses to see what jumps out. Maria will see what she can find about your ex-winemaker's movements.'

'I may be able to help,' said Emilio, looking at Maria. 'Shane was renting a place somewhere in Stanthorpe. I'll get you the address. Also, he had a friend who sometimes came here to visit him. He might know more about his movements.'

'Do you remember the friend's name?' asked Maria.

'Not really. I think Shane used to call him Dick, or something like that. Hope that's some help.'

'It could be very useful,' replied Maria. 'Thanks.'

Suddenly there was a loud bang outside. We jumped from our seats and ran towards the front door, staring into the darkening evening outside. We could see flames shooting into the sky. The noise that accompanied it was deafening. I ran to the carpark. On the other side, Emilio's car was blazing.

'Call the fire brigade and the police,' I yelled to Maria. 'Get back inside the house.'

Emilio caught up with me. When he saw what was burning, he yelled like a demented soul. 'My car! My prize BMW is on fire! Get a bucket! Get a fire-extinguisher!'

I held him back. 'Get down on the ground,' I yelled. 'The fuel could explode any minute now.'

I pushed Emilio down then fell to the ground, my arm over his body to keep him low. He struggled to get up, so I moved to lay over his body. 'Stay down,' I shouted in his ear. 'It could explode any moment.'

'No! No! No!' he moaned. 'Why? Why?'

Tears flowed down his face and his voice burbled in anguish.

I felt for him, but it was only a car. It could be replaced. A life could not.

With a resounding BANG! The fuel exploded sending flames and clouds of smoke into the air. Emilio struggled and cried out, but I continued to hold him down.

Then we heard the siren screaming as the fire engine approached. It drove into the carpark and came to a stop. Heavily clothed officers wearing hard hats and face masks jumped from the vehicle and grabbed equipment from the storage compartments.

I stood and helped Emilio to his feet. We watched as one officer, whom I took to be their leader, approached the car, and began issuing instructions. The team obeyed him with precise actions. I was impressed with their efficiency.

One officer prised the bonnet up. Two officers brought foam units to spray the engine area. This would exclude oxygen from the burning fuel and oil, to dampen down the fire in that area. Others grabbed hoses and attached them to the water taps to provide water to expand the foam and increase its efficiency once it was applied.

Soon another siren sounded, and a police car drove into the carpark, coming to a stop behind the fire truck. Two officers walked around it, keeping away from the blazing car as they approached the building. They saw us, raced over, and told us to move back inside.

As we entered, Mia hurried over to check that Emilio was okay. He hugged her with tears in his eyes. She led him to a chair, sat beside him, her hand on his arm, and gestured for Maria and I to join them.

The senior police officer went towards the fire brigade officers. The other policeman followed us inside and took a notebook from his pocket. He walked around the room jotting down the names of all the people present.

The senior officer came into the room as he was recording Mia and Emilio's name, and mine. He approached us and asked us to tell him what had happened.

Emilio was too choked up to speak so I took the role of spokesman and related the events as I had observed them. I explained that we had been seated at a table eating our dinner when we heard a loud explosion. We had run out the door to see the car in flames.

'Did you see anyone or any unusual car leaving the scene?' he asked.

'No, no one,' I replied.

Maria chimed in to say that she had heard a car rapidly accelerating just before the explosion.

'You have good ears, Miss,' he complimented.

She smiled faintly.

'Do you have any idea who might have been responsible?' he asked.

We shook our heads.

'Do you know anyone with a grudge? Is there anyone you have upset recently?'

Emilio spoke up for the first time. 'I recently had to sack a winemaker.'

'What is his name?' the officer asked.

'Shane Mason,' he answered.

'Where does he live?'

'Somewhere in Stanthorpe. I can get his address from the files. Just a moment.'

Emilio walked towards his office. I indicated with my head that Maria should follow and help him. She nodded and turned to go with him.

They soon returned with Shane's address.

The policeman nodded his thanks and noted the address in his notebook. Maria recorded it in her head.

'We will write up the report tomorrow morning. Would you be able to come to the station to read and sign the report?' he asked Emilio. 'Once you have the report number, you can contact your insurance company.'

'We will be there,' I replied.

Emilio looked at me with thanks in his eyes. He was too much in shock to speak again.

I looked through the doorway as they left. The fire was out, and the fire engine had gone. Just a mangled pile of steel lay in the carpark.

# Chapter Nine

The following morning, I was given the keys to a winery vehicle. Emilio entered the passenger seat. We fastened our seat belts and set off for Stanthorpe Police Station.

'Can I help you?' asked a cheerful female voice from behind the counter.

I explained why we were there and soon one of the officers we had met the previous evening directed us to a small meeting room. He lay a printed copy of his report on the table between us.

'Could you please read that and, if it is correct, sign at the bottom.'

Emilio and I read the report and signed it. I took out my phone to record the report number.

'Let's get you home,' I said to Emilio. 'Now you have the report number you can contact your insurance company and ask for an inspector to come and view the damage. You should have a new car quickly.'

Emilio said very little as we travelled. He was still upset over the incident. These things just didn't happen in his life. I had seen this kind of incident before. I knew the processes that had to be followed.

I handed Emilio over to Jane with the report number and instructions to contact the insurance company.

I picked up my leather jacket and helmet and walked out to my bike with my map of the district in hand. I was soon on my way to the first of my wineries for the day.

Before long, I arrived at the Lonely Dog winery. It was set back from the road and surrounded with a well-kept garden. Inside was a long timber bar decorated with a range of their wines. I was greeted with a smile by an older woman.

'Good morning, Sir,' she said. 'What kind of wine do you like?

'Good wine,' I answered with a smile.

'We have plenty of that,' she said in a definite voice. 'Browse our wine list and make a choice.'

I looked down the list and chose a white and a red. She found the wines, and a couple of tasting glasses and began her sales pitch.

I tried the two wines and made appropriate comments. Then I shifted the conversation to local matters, attempting to gauge her opinion of some of the other wineries. I began by asking her what she thought of the winemaker Emilio had sacked.

'A fool,' she answered shortly. 'He's a gambler and has got himself heavily into debt.'

'What kind of gambling?' I asked probing.

'Oh, you know. The sort you can do on your phone,' she replied.

'How do you know that?' I asked.

'My assistant, Jack Reynolds, used to share a rental flat with him,' she answered. 'He was disgusted with the way his flatmate lost his money, then asked for a loan.'

'I hope he didn't give him money.'

'Not him. He's too sensible,' she replied. 'I did hear that the winemaker came into some money recently, but that quickly disappeared into the bookies pockets.'

*I wonder if that was Emilio's money*, I thought.

I thanked her and made my exit. I was soon on my bike heading to the next winery on my list.

The name of the next winery, *Strange Bird Wine,* fascinated me. As I rode, I wondered how its name came about. When I reached the building, I was entranced by the large graphics of the strangest looking birds you could imagine, painted on the walls.

Inside I found large wireframed statues of more strange birds. I was intrigued.

A smiling attendant stood behind the bar at the end of the room. I was aware of her watching me as I walked around viewing and photographing some of these weird creatures.

'Can I help you,' she enquired.

As I walked towards the bar, I said, 'I half expected you would be dressed in a strange bird costume too.'

'I sometimes do,' she said, a wide grin spreading from ear to ear. 'But only when I wake up in a crazy mood.'

'Hope I catch that one day,' I said echoing her grin. 'But I must ask you to explain.'

'Delighted to,' she said. 'Take a seat at the bar and I'll explain it all.'

I guessed she had done this many times, but she still seemed to take pleasure in repeating the performance. *A true artist*, I thought.

'The Granite Belt is noted for being a different wine region to others in Australia,' she began. 'One of those differences is related to our rarefied climate, high in the mountains of southern Queensland. A number of grape varieties that are not grown very much in other parts of the country, do well in this area.'

She pointed to the rows of bottles on the shelf behind her. 'On these shelves you will see varieties that fall into the less than 1 percent of the Australian wine crop category. These are what we call the Strange Birds.'

I began reading the variety names from some of the bottles. Several were names I had never heard of before. Others were vaguely familiar to me, but certainly not often seen on wineshop shelves. Never had I heard of white wines called Alvarinho, Fiano or Roussanne. Nor was I familiar with red wines called Durif, Tannat or Tinto Cao.

'Okay. I'm lost,' I admitted. 'Which are your favourites?'

'Many of them,' she said.

'Just pour me a taste of one white and one red,' I asked.

She turned and walked along the shelves choosing. She selected one of each and poured a small quantity into tasting glasses.

'This is the Fiano. It is good with seafood or white meats like chicken or pork.'

I tasted it. *An interesting flavour*, I thought. 'I would like that with a prawn dish,' I said.

She nodded.

I liked the red wine too. 'I'll take a bottle of that one please,' I said. 'I'll try that with a pasta dish.'

'Good thinking,' she replied and prepared a bottle for me to take.

'What do you do when you are not playing with strange birds,' I asked.

'You probably won't believe me, but I like sword fighting.'

'Sword fighting?' I asked in total surprise. 'Where can you do that?'

'We have a mediaeval group in Stanthorpe,' she replied. 'We put on demonstrations from time to time.'

'Do you dress up and paint yourselves for that?' I enquired.

'Of course,' she replied. 'It's all theatre.'

'Must come and watch sometime,' I commented.

'We'll be performing during the Australian Small Winemakers' Show. Come and join us,' she suggested. 'It's lots of fun.'

'I have an objection to being run through by a length of sharp steel,' I replied as I picked up my bottle of wine. 'By the way, if you think your winery needs auditing, give me a call.'

I handed her a business card and left the tasting room.

# Chapter Ten

When I returned to Emilio's winery, I found Maria talking to a young woman in a school uniform.

'Come and meet Antonio's girlfriend, Bella,' she called.

I walked over and held out my hand. 'I'm very pleased to meet you, Bella. I'm sure that Maria has told you we are trying to find Antonio.'

Bella took my hand softly, her eyes showed she was not sure if I could be trusted.

Maria spoke up. 'Bella, Sean, and I have solved several crimes together in South Australia. We think we can solve this mystery too, fairly quickly.'

Maria looked at me. 'Bella came to find out where Antonio is. She is surprised he hasn't contacted her. She spoke with his parents, and they suggested she talk with us. She is concerned about Antonio's disappearance and would like to help in the search.'

'We can do with all the help we can muster,' I said. 'Can I ask you a few questions first?'

She nodded.

'Where were you when Antonio disappeared?' I asked.

'I was on a school camp that week,' she explained. 'When I came home, I was surprised he had not left any messages for me. When I checked my laptop, I found strange messages in my Messenger account. I'm frightened. I don't know what is going on.' Tears gathered in her eyes. 'I want to help find him,' she blurted out loudly.

'What resources do you have?' I asked.

'Resources?' she queried.

'Ways you can help the search,' I explained.

'I have lots of classmates who will help look for him,' she answered.

My mind wrapped itself around that thought.

*Lots of bodies who can move quickly, communicate with their phones and computers and travel freely*, I thought.

I smiled widely. 'Bella, they certainly can help us.' I turned to Maria. 'Your thoughts?'

She smiled. She liked to be included in decision-making. 'I was thinking that perhaps they could keep an eye on the winemaker, Shane Mason.'

'Good idea,' I replied.

I turned to Bella. 'We have some questions we would like answered about Shane Mason. He was recently sacked from this winery and might have been involved in Antonio's disappearance. We would like to know for instance, who does he meet, where does he shop and what does he buy? It is possible he could be buying food for

Antonio and taking it to him in a secret place. If so, where is that secret place?'

Maria chimed in. 'Do you think your friends can observe him without being noticed?'

She looked at us, a wide smile beginning to crease her face. She became excited. 'Of course, they can.'

She hopped from her chair and began dancing around. 'They are very good at doing stuff without the teacher noticing, so spying on this winemaker guy will be easy,' she added.

'Get them to text you with his every movement,' said Maria. 'Can you record their messages and relay them on to me? I will create a database that will help us create a full picture.'

'Easy,' Bella said. 'No problem.'

'Another thing,' I added. 'If they discover him taking food to Antonio, tell them not to try to rescue him. That is a job for the police. I will talk to the police and have them ready to step in and arrest the villain. What has been happening is a crime and must be punished by the law. We can help the police find the victim and the villain, but we can't make arrests. Please make this very clear to your classmates.'

Bella nodded.

Maria gave her Mason's address and Bella left quickly with a wide smile on her face. She obviously liked being involved in the search.

'We have made her happy,' I said to Maria. 'Her chums may make some valuable discoveries. It's good to have a group of Super Sleuths on the job.'

'Super Sleuths,' said Maria with a wide grin. 'I will suggest she uses that name for them. I'm sure it will appeal to them.'

We both laughed at the vision of a group of young Sherlock Holmes creeping around the countryside, pipes in their mouths and magnifying glasses held to their eyes as they searched for clues.

'Time for some more sleuthing of my own,' I said.

Before long I was on my bike and heading for yet another winery.

* * *

Soon I entered the gateway of Donna's Delights winery. The building was attractively painted and suited its name perfectly.

I walked into the Cellar Door sales area to see a man busily straightening wine bottles and dusting counters and shelves as he went. He noticed me entering the door and immediately put down his duster and grabbed a wine list for me.

'Come and sit yourself on one of these stools,' he invited. 'Was that a motorbike I heard?' he asked in a friendly manner.

'Certainly was,' I answered with a smile.

'I used to ride,' he said, 'until the wife got cranky, and I had to sell it. Pity really, but I suppose I was past my riding prime.'

'A shame,' I sympathised. 'I still find it lots of fun.'

'I don't suppose you are the auditor chap I have been hearing about,' he asked.

'How did you hear about that?' I asked, surprise on my face.

'Word gets around. The grapevine in this part of our great brown land is alive and well. I also heard you are staying in one of those Cabernet Cabins.'

Now I was really surprised. *How could that information get around?*

'They are quite comfortable.'

'I've never been inside one,' he said, 'but I must do that one day.'

He paused for a moment or two choosing his words carefully. 'There is something else I heard.'

I looked at him closely, wondering what else was general knowledge.

'I heard that you are investigating the disappearance of Emilio's son, Antonio,' he said, looking closely at me for my reaction.

'Where has that come from?'

'The owner of the Cabernet Cabins has a loose tongue. He said that Emilio made the booking for you, so it just makes sense.'

'Who has he been wagging his tongue to?' I asked, holding my breath as I waited to find out who the rumour monger was.

'Why, the owner of Tin Town Fine Dining, of course. John Marshall sees himself as the font of all secret knowledge in this part of the country. I heard you went into his restaurant for a meal the other day.'

My mouth dropped open. It almost seemed as if someone was counting my breaths when I breathed in.

'If you have heard all of that, I don't suppose you have heard where Antonio is?' I asked almost as a joke.

'Can't help you with that,' he replied, although I believed he would love to pass on that information if he knew it.

'Well, if you find out, could you give me a tingle?' I asked as I passed over one of my business cards.

He took the card and read it carefully.

'So, you really are an auditor,' he said. 'I thought it was just a blind.'

'A blind for what?' I asked. I was intrigued with the fact these stories had been spread about me.

'Oh, a private detective or something,' he blustered.

'Sorry to disappoint you. I really am an auditor. Emilio is cousin to a friend of mine in Adelaide and I was asked to sort out his money worries. I will be auditing his business. Then I will move on to Harmony winery. After that I could do yours if you wanted.'

He looked at me with interest. 'We could do with a once over of our business. I'll talk with Donna and get back to you.'

He remembered his purpose in this winery tasting room. 'Would you like to try some of our wines?'

'I'll leave that until I come to do your audit,' I said with a smile. 'By the way, I have a tidbit of gossip for you to spread around.'

His face beamed with interest. He leaned forward across the bar, his ears almost flapping with impatience.

'Antonio's sweetheart is the Tin Town Fine Dining owner's daughter, Bella.'

His face lit up like a bright star. 'Dinky-di?' he queried.

'Dinky-di!' I responded.

'Wow. The boys will love that tidbit.' He laughed out loud. 'Thank you for telling me.'

'Tit for tat,' I responded as I turned towards the door.

*I must get back to tell Maria about all this*, I thought. *I need to be very careful, or I could be the next one firebombed.*

# Chapter Eleven

Back at Emilio's winery, I sought Maria. I found her still engrossed with her laptop searches.

'Time for us to talk,' I said.

'Just a moment,' was her reply. 'I need to save some notes I have been writing.'

'See you outside,' I said and left the room.

A short while later she joined me. 'What have you discovered?' she asked.

'Heaps. I have been found out. The owner of Tin Town Fine Dining has been spreading the rumour that I am here to find Antonio. The owner of the Cabernet Cabins told him Emilio made the booking for me. So, now I will be a target, and so will you by association.'

'Oh! That is terrible,' she said, her face reflecting her concern. 'What can we do?'

'Find Antonio as quickly as we can. What have you discovered?' I asked.

'Firstly, I have found the winemaker's phone number and I have been reading some of his text messages. He has been texting his friend Dirk. I have copied some of those you might like to read.'

'How can you do that?'

'By magic, of course,' she said smiling at me.

I liked her beautiful smile. 'I'm pleased to be working with a magician,' I said, partly in awe. 'Remind me to buy you a cape and a wand.'

She laughed. 'I have some software that helps me decode the messages after I find the number.'

'I thought it would be something sneaky like that. What else have you discovered?'

'The Super Sleuths are already on the job.'

'Already?'

'Already. Bella reports that some of them followed Shane Mason into the supermarket and recorded that he bought breakfast cereal and milk, some fruit, and several instant dinners.'

'For himself or Antonio?' I asked.

'We don't know, but then he went to a hardware store and bought some plant fertilizer.'

'Did it have ammonium nitrate in it, did they say?'

'The report says he doesn't have a garden so I think we can assume it was to build a firebomb. Then he went to a service station and bought a can of diesel.'

'Definitely for a bomb,' I stated. 'Are we in danger again?'

'I think we have always been in danger,' said Maria. 'We'll just have to be very careful.'

She continued, 'Bella's report goes on.'

I listened closely. Things were turning very nasty.

'Our winemaker then went to a pub to meet his mate, Dirk. They had a couple of beers, then put their heads close together and had a quiet conversation,' finished Maria.

'Oh, to be a fly on the wall,' I said. 'Our Super Sleuths are doing a great job so far. Did Bella like the name?'

'She was ecstatic about the name and spread it among her group of sleuthing friends. She said they are delighted to be likened to Sherlock Holmes.'

'I think we should ask them to put a tail on Shane's mate, Dirk, as well.'

'I've already suggested that to her,' said Maria. 'Hope that was okay.'

'Thank you. I love working with you,' I said. 'You are the smartest partner I've ever had.'

I put my hand on her shoulder and gave her a pat. She reached up and grasped my hand.

'And I love working with you,' she said. 'You always compliment me when I do something to please you.'

My phone rang, interrupting us. I answered the call, 'Yes, Sean speaking.'

'I know where Antonio is,' said the caller in a gruff voice.

I was stunned for a moment.

'Who's calling?'

'Just call me Fred. I know you are looking for Antonio and I can tell you where he is.'

The caller paused.

'Where is he?'

'Can't talk now. Meet me at 9 pm at the Rainbow Winery.'

The call was closed.

'Whew!' I said, 'The caller said he knows where Antonio is. He said I should meet him at the Rainbow Winery tonight at 9 pm.'

'Do you trust him?' Maria asked. Her eyes reflected the doubt in her mind.

'Not at all. But it could be worth checking out,' I said, my mind jumping between two camps labelled TRUE and FALSE.

'You're crazy. That sounds like a scam to lure you.'

'I think you are right, but we have to check out every possibility.'

'You are crazy,' she shouted, 'but if you go, I am coming with you.'

'You're crazy, too,' I replied, 'but I'd feel happier with you along.'

'Do you have a gun?' she asked. 'We need something to protect us.'

'No, but I am good at Karate,' I said. 'We'll ask Emilio if he has a gun we can borrow. Can you shoot?'

'I've practised on a range many times. Marcello insisted on it.'

'Well done, Marcello. That is something I didn't know about him,' I finished.

Later that night we dressed in dark clothing and leather jackets. Maria had a small pistol hidden in her jacket pocket within easy reach. We pulled on our helmets and mounted the bike.

It was a pleasant night. The moon shone brightly, lighting up the countryside with a lovely glow.

We rode along the main highway, seeing very little traffic at this time of night. Eventually, I turned into the side road that would take us into the Rainbow Winery. Trees grew thickly on both sides of the road making it seem as if we were riding along a tunnel. I slowed the bike, travelling at a snail's pace. I hadn't been along this road before, so I was unsure of its twists and turns.

Suddenly, Maria's arms around my body tightened as she shouted, 'Duck!'

We both tucked our heads down onto our chests. I felt a ping on the top of my helmet as if something was trying to grab me.

I heard Maria call, 'Stop.'

I pulled the bike to a stop.

'Are you okay?' I shouted through my mask.

'Yes,' she shouted back. 'Are you okay?'

'I think so, but what was attacking us?'

'A taut wire,' she called in a muffled voice.

We tumbled from the bike and removed out helmets and masks.

We walked back a few steps and saw a taut length of fencing wire stretched across the road at what would have been our neck height.

Someone wanted to take our heads off, I realised. 'Glad you saw it in time,' I complimented.

'The moonlight was glistening off it,' she said. 'That is the closest I have come to death.'

I noticed she had begun trembling. Her body shook with fright and fear. I put my arms around her and pulled her in tightly. She rested her head on my chest but continued shaking so I began patting her back and crooning soothing words, almost like reassuring a young child.

While I held her, I searched the area for signs of movements and listened for the sound of anyone approaching. All was quiet.

After a while, the shaking grew less, and she lifted her head to me. I bent mine down and our lips met in a deep and heartfelt kiss. Then she snuggled back into my shoulder for another moment.

Finally, she lifted her head and looked into my eyes. 'Sean, I want to come home with you tonight.'

'Are you sure,' I asked quietly.

She just nodded.

'Okay,' I replied and hugged her tightly for a few more moments.

Checking for signs of movements, I said, 'Let's sort out this mess, then we'll be on our way before someone comes to check if they were successful.'

Reluctantly, she stepped back, and I took out my phone. I began filming the wire. She followed me as I moved to one end and took shots of where it was attached to a stout tree. Then we walked into the scrub on the other side and eventually located the wire tensioning tool I knew would be there.

After some camera shots, still wearing my gloves, I freed the tension from the wire and the tool came loosely into my hands. Once disconnected, the wire fell to the ground.

'We need this for fingerprints,' I said.

I placed the tool in one of the panier bags on the back of the bike and quickly rolled up the wire, leaving it in a heap well off the road.

'How did you know about that?' asked Maria, obviously impressed with the way I knew how to disconnect the taut wire so quickly.

'Lots of experience on a farm,' I replied offhandedly. 'I'll tell you all about it one day.'

'Oh,' was the only response I got.

'We'll take the wire tensioner to the police tomorrow for them to check for fingerprints. Hopefully, they'll come up with a match. Now, let's get you home where you can shower and begin to feel alive again.'

We mounted the bike and made good time back to the cabin. I could feel Maria's arms holding me tightly as we travelled.

# Chapter Twelve

Once inside the cabin, I helped Maria remove her heavy leather coat, helmet, and gloves, then pointed her towards the shower.

'Towels are in the large drawer next to the shower,' I said.

She smiled and walked to the bathroom, closing the door behind her.

I walked out to the bike, retrieved the fence tensioner with my gloved hands and came back to find a large plastic bag to store it in.

I took off my heavy outer clothing, set the table for breakfast and attended to other household chores.

Sometime later, Maria came out of the bathroom with a heavy towel wrapped around her.

'Which way to the bedroom?' she asked.

I pointed her in the right direction.

'Your turn for a shower,' she said pointedly.

I nodded and walked to the bathroom to take my shower.

Before long I left the bathroom with a heavy towel around me and walked to the bedroom.

*  *  *

Later in the night, a loud roar woke me. I jumped from the bed and raced out to the living area. A bright glow shone through the rear windows and sparks flew high into the sky. The back cabin was ablaze.

I grabbed my phone and called the fire brigade and the police. Then I ran back into the bedroom and woke Maria.

'Grab some clothes,' I yelled. 'The back cabin is on fire.'

I dressed rapidly and ran outside. I wheeled the motorbike away from the inferno and found a garden hose. I turned the tap on full and directed the stream at the edge of the blaze. The radiated heat prevented me from getting too close.

Maria ran out to help me with a hat in her hands. She pulled it onto my head.

'That will give you a little protection,' she said.

'Thanks,' I muttered then heard the wail of a siren.

The fire engine soon pulled up and the team bundled out of the vehicle, hurrying to do their preparations. In next to no time, they had a powerful blast of water directed at the worst of the blaze. They were experts, knowing how and where to direct their efforts.

It wasn't long before a police vehicle drove into the park.

'Not you again!' shouted an exasperated policeman. 'Do you start these things or is a firebug following you around?'

'It's a firebug, and I think I know who he is,' I said quickly.

He looked at me with a closed expression on his face. 'You think you know who did it? Tell me who.'

'The same man who burnt Emilio's car, Shane Mason, the ex-winemaker at Top of the Range Winery.'

'Why do you think it was him?'

'He has a grudge against Emilio, and me, because I'm checking who took the money from the winery account. We also know that yesterday he bought ammonium nitrate fertilizer and diesel, the two main ingredients in a firebomb.'

The policeman looked at me, not sure whether to believe me or not, but knowing that the story sounded plausible.

'We need to have a big talk with you tomorrow when you come in to sign the report.'

He made some notes in his notebook.

'Tomorrow, I need to speak with your sergeant. What is his name?' I asked.

'Sergeant Bill Masterson. Why do you need to talk with him?' the policeman asked. By his worried expression I think he was concerned that I was going to complain about his behaviour.

'Last evening, someone tried to kill us.'

The policeman took a long, deep look at me, then moved his gaze to Maria. 'Care to explain?' he asked.

'Not now,' I replied. 'When I come in tomorrow, I will bring the evidence.'

'We tried to contact the owner of these cabins, but he was not answering his phone,' said the policeman. 'We'll try again in the morning. We'll see you tomorrow as well.' He went over to talk to the Fire Brigade officer then turned and called to his team who were poking around the burnt cabin, 'Come on boys. We'll come back in the morning. Too dark to see anything now.'

They piled into the police car and drove off. By this time, the fire brigade had extinguished the blaze and were beginning to collect their equipment and store it back in the truck.

'It appears it was deliberately lit. We will be back tomorrow to look for evidence. But it is safely out and shouldn't give you any more trouble,' their leader said to me. 'It is probably safe for you to go back to bed, unless you are worried the firebomber will come back.'

'Thank you very much. As it's nearly dawn, I think we will take our chances,' I said reaching out my hand to give his hand a strong shake. 'We thank you for your amazing efforts from the bottom of our hearts.'

'All in a night's work,' he said with a smile. 'Glad to have been of service.'

'You deserve a medal,' said Maria quietly. 'Thank you.'

He smiled again then turned to climb into the fire truck. He gave a wave as they drove out of the car park onto the road.

* * *

Mid-morning the next day, we climbed onto the Bike and set off for Stanthorpe. The fence tensioner in its plastic bag was safely tucked into one of the panier bags over the back wheels.

Before long, we pulled up at the front of the police station. We approached the front desk and when asked what we wanted, I explained we needed to see the sergeant.

'What about, Sir?' the young female officer on the desk asked.

'An attempted murder.'

'Who was the intended victim?' she asked.

'Us,' I replied.

'Oh. Give me a moment and I will see if he is free,' she said.

She lifted the phone on her desk and dialled a number. When the call was answered, she explained our reason for wanting to see him. She listened, then said, "Yes, Sarg. I will do that.'

She rose from her desk and said, 'Please follow me.'

She took us to a closed door at the end of the corridor and knocked.

'Come,' we heard.

She opened the door and ushered us in.

'Good morning,' said Sergeant Bill Masterson. 'Please tell me your names.'

'Sean O'Connor,' I said.

'An Irishman, eh?' he said as he wrote my name down.

'As Irish as Paddy McGinty's goat,' I said with a grin, 'but now a true-blue Aussie.'

He smiled, then looked at Maria.

'Maria Antonucci,' she said, adding, 'another true-blue Aussie.'

He smiled again and wrote down her name alongside mine.

He looked up and asked, 'What is this about an attempted murder?'

I explained our search for Antonio and the strange phone call that lured us to the side road leading to the Rainbow Winery. Then I described our ride along this deserted road and the wire strung tightly across the road at the height of our throats. Then I looked at Maria.

'I spotted moonlight reflecting off the wire, and shouted to Sean to duck his head,' said Maria. 'We both ducked and felt the wire glancing off the tops of our helmets.'

The sergeant was captivated with her description. He leaned forward, waiting for more.

When she paused, he said impatiently, 'Then?'

'We dismounted and followed the wire into the scrub until we found the tensioner,' I added. 'I released the tension and disconnected the wire.'

'This is a gripping story, but I have to asked for evidence,' said the sergeant.

I pulled out my camera, opened the photo section and found the most recent shots. I handed the phone over the desk. The sergeant looked closely at the shots, pausing at one then moving on.

'Any other evidence,' he asked.

I reached to the package beside my chair and handed the wire tensioner in its plastic bag across the desk.

'I only handled this with gloves on so there may be useful fingerprints on it.'

'You're not a detective?' he asked.

'No,' I replied, 'but I have helped the South Australian police with several enquiries. So has Maria.'

He looked at me, unsure whether to believe me.

'Please call Detective Inspector Ken Harris at the Adelaide Crime Investigation Branch. He will vouch for me.'

I printed his name and number on a desk pad and handed it to him.

The sergeant lifted his phone and dialled the number. After a few moments, he said, 'Can I please speak with Detective Inspector Ken Harris.'

Someone obviously asked for his details, and he replied, 'Sergeant Bill Masterson from the Stanthorpe Police Station, Queensland.'

The call was put through, and he was soon speaking with my mate Ken Harris. He and I went back a long time.

'I have someone here who says he knows you,' he explained.

He was obviously asked who he was referring to.

'He says his name is Sean O'Connor.'

He listened for a few moments then put his phone on speaker.

'Hi, Sean,' said my mate, Ken Harris. 'Getting yourself into trouble again.'

'Just a few fire bombings and someone trying to take my head off, Ken,' I said loudly.

'Nothing serious then,' he replied and laughed. 'Sounds normal for you. You just take care. I don't want my best mate to come to grief. Do you have someone to look out for you?

'I have Maria Antonucci who is a very good watch dog.'

'Is she from Adelaide?' he asked.

'Yes, Ken.'

'Is she good with computers?'

'Yes, she is.'

'Well, I'm guessing who she might be. If I am right, you are in very good hands. Put me back to the sergeant.'

I nodded to the sergeant, and he took the phone off speaker. He listened intently then placed the phone down.

'I believe you two can help us. Let's talk business.'

# Chapter Thirteen

'Okay. Let's start at the beginning,' said the sergeant looking at me.

I began, 'Emilio, the owner of Top of the Range Winery is missing both his son, Antonio, and lots of money from his accounts. As a business auditor I was asked to investigate the loss of money by a good friend of mine, Emilio's cousin, who lives in Adelaide. I was also asked to investigate the disappearance of his son, Antonio.'

I handed the sergeant one of my business cards.

'I'm not sure Antonio's disappearance has been reported to us,' said the sergeant. He checked his computer files. 'No. Can we please have a formal report filed at the desk?'

'He's definitely missing and there is some evidence we can submit,' I said. 'I will see it is done.'

'Thank you. Please continue.'

'I found that Emilio had recently sacked his winemaker, Shane Mason, because of the expensive loss of wine through his inattention, but this person still had access to Emilio's bank account, and by all accounts also has a gambling addiction. I had Emilio change the password to his account to stop any further losses.'

I took a breath. 'I believe that Shane Mason was incensed when Emilio's bank accounts were no longer available to him, so he firebombed Emilio's car. Then he found that I was helping Emilio sort out his accounts and firebombed the cabin.'

'Why did he firebomb the wrong cabin?

'Because I misled the rumour monger in this town, John Marshall.'

'Please explain?' said the sergeant.

'When I went to Tin Town Fine Dining for a meal, John Marshall quizzed me too closely and I became suspicious. He wanted to know which cabin I was in, so I told him the back one.'

'And that was the one that was firebombed?'

'Exactly.'

'So, Marshall is partly responsible for the fire? Let me see what we have on file about those fires.'

The sergeant tapped in his computer and read the reports entered by his officers.

'So, we have a firebombed vehicle one night and a firebombed cabin the next night. Quite a coincidence when Emilio Angelica and then the person helping him investigate his losses are both targeted.'

He turned to Maria. 'I see you told the attending police that Shane Mason had the means to do it. Can you tell me how you know he had bought the ingredients for a firebomb?'

She smiled at finally being included. 'Our Super Sleuths followed him to observe his buying spree.'

'Super Sleuths? Who are you talking about?'

She smiled again. 'Antonio's girlfriend Bella Marshall came to see us and asked for help in finding Antonio. According to her Messenger messages, it seems he was grabbed in Stanthorpe, and nobody has heard from him since. She said her school chums were keen to help find him, so we suggested they spy on Shane Mason as a first step. They followed him as he went shopping and reported on all his purchases. They reported back to Bella, and she reported to me.'

'So, we have a herd of school students spying on people? This is highly illegal and dangerous. They are outside the law.'

'They have a highly developed sense of civic duty and law and order,' I butted in. 'I'm sure some of them will consider a career in the police force as a result of these experiences.'

'Humphhh! What is Mason's address?'

'It was given to the police at the car fire. It's 110a Thomas Street, Stanthorpe,' said Maria.

The Sergeant went to the door and opened it. 'Steve,' he called.

When Steve arrived, the sergeant said, 'Why wasn't Shane Mason brought in for questioning after the car was firebombed?'

'We talked to him, and he had an alibi for the time of the fire. We had no evidence to suspect it was him.'

'We might well be able to gather evidence now. Take the paddy wagon and a couple of the troops to 110a Thomas St., Stanthorpe. Arrest Shane Mason on one count of firebombing a car, and one count of firebombing a building. Get Sally to print out a Search Warrant for his house and bring it to me for a signature. You are looking for any signs of bomb making tools and ingredients, in particular ammonium nitrate fertilizer and diesel with strips of cotton for a fuse. You might also look for signs of addiction to gambling. This should have been done last time.'

Steve went red and muttered, 'Will do, Sarg. Sorry. We didn't think it was him.'

The sergeant waved a hand at him as if he was shooing a fly, then came back into the room. He stood at the door until the search warrant was brought to him for signing. He scribbled a signature and closed the door again.

'Next,' he said. 'What about the boy, Antonio? Who would want to abduct him?'

Maria answered, 'When I got into Antonio's laptop, I found that someone had altered Bella's Facebook Messenger conversation with Antonio. Do you know what Facebook Messenger is?' she asked politely.

'I do,' he said with a smile. 'My wife and son both use it.'

'Bella's very last message wasn't in her normal language or tone. It said she was in terrible trouble and needed lots of money, and Antonio should meet her at the school bus stop near her father's restaurant two nights later. I think someone else wrote that last message.'

'Who do you think might have written it?'

'We think it might have been her mother who we believe has been trying to discourage her friendship with Antonio.'

'What reason would she have for doing that?'

'I suspect she wanted to discourage a relationship with an Italian boy.'

'You think she is racist?' he asked.

'Possibly.'

'If she captured Antonio, she couldn't do it alone. Who could have helped her?' the sergeant posed.

'We haven't found an answer to that yet. That is our next priority.'

'If they killed him, we should have recovered a body by now,' said the sergeant. 'If they have hidden him away, they would have to feed him so someone delivering food should have been seen. Thank you both for being straight up and honest with me. I think we can work together as your friend the Detective Inspector suggests, but please keep me in the loop.'

He showed us to the door. 'I'll let you know if we find a match for the fingerprints on that wire tensioner.'

We walked through the station to the door, then down the steps to the footpath. I suggested we go for a coffee at the Tin Town Fine Dining so she could meet John Marshall.

We walked in and Marshall seemed surprised to see me.

'Can we please have two flat white coffees,' I asked.

He jotted down the order then looked at Maria.

'Who are you?' he asked inquisitively.

I introduced her. 'This is Jane from England.'

'You look Italian to me,' he said rudely.

'And you look German,' she said just as rudely, her beautiful face twisting into an angry mask. 'Germans did terrible things to my family in the last war, and I don't like Germans.'

She looked at me. 'I don't want to drink his coffee,' she said loudly, her hair swinging around her head to emphasize her rejection. 'It will probably poison us.'

Marshall took a step or two backwards in shock. He wasn't used to people standing up to him.

We moved to the door, but as we opened it to escape, I saw him reach for his phone. I looked at my watch and noted the time. It was 1.17pm.

'He didn't like that,' I commented as we headed for the bike. 'Well done.'

'I hate him,' she exploded. 'Don't let me near him ever again!'

I wasn't used to her expressing her thoughts with so much venom. I took her hand and kissed it.

Before long we were on the bike ready to head home.

'Can we go to see Emilio first?' asked Maria. 'He needs to know what has happened. Besides, I need my laptop and some clean clothes.'

'Of course,' I replied as I headed for Top of the Range Winery.

# Chapter Fourteen

As we rode at the speed limit, I looked in the rear-view mirror and noticed a black saloon coming up behind us very fast.

*This could be trouble*, I thought.

'Hold on tight,' I called to Maria. 'I think we are being chased. If I have to make a turn, bend with the bike and my body. Don't bend the other way or you will upset us.'

'Okay,' she called bravely.

*She's a keeper*, I thought.

The car was upon us in moments. It drew abreast and then swung towards us, obviously trying to put the bike in the ditch and us in our coffins.

Maria saw what the car was trying to do and clung to me tightly, expecting me to know how to deal with it.

'That's your game, is it?' I shouted, more to bring my body to fever pitch and awaken every sense than just defiance.

I flattened the bike, and we were soon speeding along at way over the speed limit. I shot ahead of the car and saw it falling back in our private race.

The driver realised what I had done and increased his speed. Before long he was slowly catching up.

Staying well ahead of him so he couldn't ram us, I began swinging the bike in half curves, in and out of the central road markings to stop him trying to get alongside.

He pressed his hand on the horn button, as he tried to catch up, attempting to make me lose my concentration.

In my youth, I used to race at bike events where noise came from every quarter. Crowds shouted, car horns blared, official bells and whistles indicated various stages of every race. Music shouted from large speakers. I had learned in those days to completely ignore the cacophony and concentrate on the race. A blaring car horn was nothing to my practiced ear.

In the distance, I saw we were approaching a large bend in the road. I knew this was a sharp and potentially dangerous bend to take at speed. I kept my speed up to entice the car driver into watching me, not the road ahead.

As we entered the bend, I bent my right knee out to grab the wind that would help us turn and rolled the bike over. We lent over so far that my right foot peg was almost scraping the road. Luckily, Maria bent with me. She was a quick learner.

Once around the bend, I straightened up, slowed right down and then stopped when we heard a mighty crash. We looked back. The car hadn't been able to take the bend at that speed. It had rolled and slid through the light scrub before crashing into a huge granite boulder.

'Better call the police and the ambulance,' I said, 'but I'm guessing there won't be anyone in that vehicle worth rescuing.'

Maria took out her phone and rang 000. When the call was answered, she said, 'Police and then Ambulance, please.' Once she was connected, she gave our names and the location of the accident.

We waited for a while until a police car arrived.

'Not you again?' spluttered the same policeman who had attended the fires at Emilio's winery and the cabin.

'Do you cause all these tragedies or has the whole world decided to rub you out?' he asked, huge questions in his voice.

I smiled. 'We seem to attract trouble. You'd better tell your Sergeant that someone else tried to murder us. I'm sure he won't be amused. See if you can identify the driver. His fingerprints could be useful.'

'Come on, Bob,' the policeman said to his mate. 'We'd better take a look at the wreck. Someone may need pulling out.'

They began wading through the tall grass to the smashed vehicle.

An ambulance pulled up and two guys in white uniforms ran into the scrub, following the policemen. After a brief inspection, one of the policemen came back and took our statement.

'Do you know who it is? Is he still alive,' I asked.

He shook his head sadly, then with the usual message to come to the station tomorrow, he said we could leave.

We remounted the bike and rode at a much safer speed back to the Top of the Range Winery.

Emilio and his family were pleased to see us alive and well.

'We heard terrible things about a fire in one of the Cabernet Cabins,' said Mia. 'We hoped it wasn't yours. Emilio tried to ring you, but we had no phone signal last night.'

'Luckily, it was the back unit, not the front one,' I replied.

Mia looked at Maria. 'We missed you last night.'

'Sorry I didn't contact you. Someone tried to murder us last night, so Sean took me home with him to protect me,' said Maria quickly.

Mia and Emilio looked at her closely, concern clearly etched on their faces.

'What is going on?' they asked, almost together.

'Someone rang with the message that if we met him in the evening, he would tell us where Antonio is,' explained Maria. 'We rode to the meeting place, but someone had stretched a length of fencing wire across the road at the height of our necks.'

She emphasised the horror of the moment by holding the edge of her hand up to her neck and moving it in and out.

Expressions of total horror crossed the faces of our hosts. Mia held her hands up in front of her face to try to block out the mental image.

I cut in, 'Maria saw the wire just in time because of moonlight reflecting off it. We ducked and saved our lives. We went back to the cabin in almost total shock.'

'Then in the middle of the night, the back cabin caught on fire. We called the fire brigade and the police. This morning we visited the police to tell them the whole story.'

'Who set fire to the cabin? Emilio asked.

'The police agree with us that it was your sacked winemaker. We are also sure he was the one who firebombed your car. When we left the station, several police had gone to arrest him.'

'Good,' said Emilio. 'Anything else we should know?' he asked.

'Yes,' said Maria. 'As we were riding here, a car tried to run us off the road and kill us.'

'Another murder attempt!' exclaimed Mia, her face showing the horror she was feeling.

'Afraid so,' I answered. 'As your winemaker is now in jail, it was someone else who tried to kill us. Fortunately, whoever it was failed to take the big bend and hit a large granite rock. You will see the remains of the vehicle if you take a trip into Stanthorpe.'

'What about the people in the car? Are they dead?' asked Mia. She held her breathe, her hand hovering near her mouth, hoping not to hear the answer she expected.

'Yes,' I replied, 'He hit the rock at full speed. I would have been surprised if they survived that crash.'

'Time for a stiff drink for the pair of you,' said Emilio as he headed towards a liquor cabinet.

'I'll drink to that,' I said predictably. 'I don't suppose you have any Irish whiskey?' I asked, almost in vain.

'No, but I have some local Italian grappa that I think is similar to your Irish poitín.'

'I'll try anything once,' I said with a smile, 'but just a small one.'

# Chapter Fifteen

We spent some time with Emilio and Mia talking about our searches for Antonio but eventually I felt it was time to return to the cabin.

'Are you sure it is safe?' Emilio asked.

I nodded with more assurance than I felt. 'Shane is in custody and the other guy is dead. Surely there is no one else out there trying to kill us. We'll be fine.' But lingering doubts clouded my I mind.

'I need to grab my laptop and some clothes before we go,' said Maria. 'I have more checking to do.'

'Not only that,' I added. 'We need to get our Super Sleuths working on some new investigations to find Antonio.'

She smiled and walked to her bedroom to grab her things. We said our goodbyes and headed back to the cabin.

Once there, Maria fired up her laptop and with her fast fingers began a message to Bella.

'What investigations do our young friends need to make?' she asked me.

I began, 'We have to assume that, as the police have not found a body, Antonio has been hidden somewhere. I would like our team to visit every place in Stanthorpe where a person could be hidden away. There are multiple caravan parks, but I'm sure there are also storage places where a shed or container can be hired.'

'There are also a number of motels in and around Stanthorpe so they should go on the list too,' added Maria.

'Can you please make a special mention of the danger,' I added. 'I don't want groups of less than three or four of our Super Sleuths to search together. There are some nasty people out there.'

Maria nodded. 'I'll make special mention of that.'

She typed away, then checked her emails.

'There's a message from my brother,' she said. 'He is missing me and watching our activities from afar. He says he is emailing me a new phone number checking modification he has written that might help us.'

I knew that Maria and her brother worked in a rarefied technological atmosphere where nothing that happened anywhere was secret.

'Who is the person we need to keep the closest watch on?' she asked.

'The police now have the sacked winemaker so the next two people I think we should watch are the winemaker's mate, Dirk Thomas, and Bella's father, John Marshall.'

'I already have John Marshall's phone number from the Tin Town Fine Dining website. I'll have to ask Google to help me find Dirk Thomas's phone number. Just a moment.'

Her finger flashed across the keyboard so fast my eyesight was blurred. Before long she smiled.

'Got it. Now I'll enter those two numbers into the new tracking software that Alonzo has sent me. Before long, I'll be able to find who they have been talking to. Not only that, but we will also know the phone numbers they called, the numbers that called them, who those numbers belong to and how long each call took.'

It sounded like mumbo jumbo to me, but this woman was smart. I had to believe she knew what she was talking about. She seemed to be able to get into databases that, I had believed, were not available to the public. Silly me.

*We are now in the hi-tech age,* I said to myself, *and it is passing me by, faster than a speeding bullet.*

My phone rang. I answered and found myself talking with Sergeant Bill Masterson.

'Hi, Sean, he said. 'We arrested Shane Mason and found evidence of firebomb making in his flat. He also pleaded guilty to stealing money from Emilio to pay his gambling debts. He thinks it might have been around $30,000. I think it could be much more. I would like that checked. He will be going away for a long time, so you don't have to worry about any more firebombs… I hope,' he added.

'I have Emilio's accountant working to establish how much money he took. We should have a final figure soon,' I said.

'Good,' said the Sergeant. 'We will need that for the court.'

He continued, 'The car that tried to run you off the road was stolen and was driven by his mate Dirk Thomas. He died in the crash, so you don't have to worry about him trying another murder attempt. By the way, his fingerprints don't match those on the wire tensioner you brought in. Neither do the fingerprints of the Rainbow Winery staff, so we have a third villain out there somewhere. Please be very careful.'

'That's two worries taken off my shoulders,' I replied. 'Just one to go. Thank you, Sergeant, for the update. Your officers have been very efficient. Please pass on my thanks.'

'What are you two up to now?' he asked. 'Still coaching your junior detectives?'

'Yes,' I answered. 'We have them checking all the places where Antonio could be hidden, like onsite caravans and storage depots. I've warned them all to travel in groups for their safety and report to you any suspicious activity.'

'If you can arrange it, Sean, I would like to speak to the group. I need to remind them of their civil rights and responsibilities, but also make some suggestions about the best way to watch and record what they see.'

'Excellent,' I commented. 'I would like to be there to remind them of how to keep themselves and each other safe.'

'Good, Sean. We are on the same page. I'll wait to hear from you about a place and time.'

He closed the call.

I told Maria the good news about the arrest and who was in the car that tried to run us off the road. She smiled and I could see the relief in her eyes.

'Unfortunately, the fingerprints on the wire tensioner didn't match either of them. So we still have to be careful,' I said, looking out the window.

'Oh, Sean, do you think we should stay? Who else would want to kill us?'

'The kidnapper, I guess. We'll stay but be careful. Oh, and the Sergeant wants to address the Super Sleuths and give them a tip or two,' I said to Maria.

'Great,' she responded. 'I'll let Bella know. I suggest we do it at the school. Would you like to speak to the principal?'

'Excellent suggestion. Can you get me his number? I'll call him right away.'

Maria tapped her keyboard and had the number in moments. I called and had an in-depth chat with the principal. He immediately agreed and suggested a time the next day. He promised to set aside a room and gave me the room number.

I called the Sergeant and gave him the date, time, and place. He thanked me for organising it so quickly.

I reached for my notebook and drafted the things I needed to say to the students about keeping them and their buddies safe.

The next afternoon, we arrived at the school a little early and made our way to the Administration block. The sergeant soon followed us. The principal guided us to the room. We made ourselves comfortable and students began filing into the room soon after.

The group included both girls and boys of about Bella's age. Their cheerful chatter died away when they saw both the principal and the police sergeant at the front of the room, and whispered conversation took its place.

Bella walked into the room and Maria waved her over to sit with us. She looked a little surprised but smiled and walked over to sit next to Maria.

I stood and they stopped talking.

'I'm Sean O'Connor. I'm an auditor of wineries and I was invited to your area to help Top of the Range sort out some money problems. I also investigate crimes. Maria is a super technical whizz who helps me with my investigations.'

The room was very quiet. This was not a normal school lesson period.

I continued, 'When we arrived in the Granite Belt last week, we found that Antonio Angelica had disappeared. Bella Marshall came to see us, and she offered your help to find him. So, you are the brave people that we decided to call the Super Sleuths.'

Smiles appeared on faces all around the room. *They like that name*, I thought.

'The Police Sergeant wants to help you fulfill that role legally, and I am keen to help you carry out your detective activities safely. Maria will talk to you about communication. Your principal has very kindly organized this time and place for us to meet, so we can show that we support what you are doing. Some of you, at a later stage in your life, may like to become real detectives. I now call upon Sergeant Bill Masterson.'

The Sergeant stood up. 'There are some legal issues you need to keep in mind when you are collecting information, and there are some tips I have about the way you observe and record what you see.'

He gave a clear and direct account of their legal liabilities when moving around and observing people. He then gave them some useful tips on watching and recording their observations. I noticed some of them writing these tips into their notebooks. He sat down.

I stood and talked about the possible dangers of following and observing people who might turn nasty if they noticed they were being observed. I advised them to always travel and observe in groups.

'Never go it alone,' I said sternly. 'We don't want any dead Super Sleuths. In fact, I would like you to move into groups of three or four or perhaps five now. I will give you a few moments to move to form your groups.'

There was a hustle and bustle as chairs scraped and bodies jostled. Before long, the students were sitting in groups.

Maria stood up. 'Bella is your communications officer,' she said. 'She communicates directly with me, and I record everything that you people see. Crimes are often solved through clear and accurate recording. It is very important that everything you observe is communicated to Bella, accurately and completely.

'It is no good saying to her, "I saw Fred buying something at the shops." We need to know, Who, When, Where and What. The four W's are all important. If you can add a fifth W, Why, then that is gold. If you can report what you observe clearly and completely to Bella, I can create a clear and informative database that will help us solve this mystery quickly.'

She sat down to a number of students hand clapping her. Soon they all joined in.

Bella stood. The group looked at her in surprise.

'Thank you all for agreeing to join in the hunt for Antonio,' she began. 'I would like each group to choose one person as their communications person. I don't want to have to deal with messages from each of you. One person from each group will make things much easier. When you have chosen, would that person please text me, so I know who I am dealing with. Give your group a name. I will allocate each group a set target to observe. Thank you,' she ended and sat down.

The students clapped her as well. We all stood, and we clapped the students. They loved that.

With wide smiles all around, we vacated the room, and the students went back to their classes. We thanked the principal for organising the meeting then left the school.

The Sergeant shook my hand and then Maria's. 'Looks like the Super Sleuths are officially launched,' he said, a wide grin on his face.

# Chapter Sixteen

We called in on Emilio on our way home. He gave a quick wave as he bustled around gathering boxes of wine together.

'What is going on?' I asked.

'I am gathering wine to take to the Australian Small Winemakers' Show,' he answered as he put down another box on the heap near the winery door.

'It begins next weekend, and we still don't have Antonio,' he said sadly. He looked at the boxes. 'Some of this wine was made by him and I am sure he will win an award or two.' He shook his head, his face grim.

Sadness and frustration vied for a place in my mind. I vowed to find the boy and bring him back. Then I offered the only thing I had to offer right now. 'Do you need a hand?' I asked.

'Thank you, but no. The boys have done this before. Once I have chosen the wines, they will load the boxes into the van and off we will go. I just need you to find my boy.'

'We are close,' I promised. 'Just a day or two more,' I said and hoped it was true.

I just hoped our Super Sleuths would turn up something in the next day or two.

'I need to get back to my laptop,' Maria said. 'My fingers are getting itchy.'

Obviously, she felt the urgency and frustration I did.

Before long we were back in the cabin, and she was tapping at the keyboard. A knock at the door took me in that direction. I peered through the window, a short guy dressed in jeans and country shirt stood there with a piece of paper in his hand. He looked harmless. Sometimes, looks can be deceiving.

I opened the door and greeted him.

I got a snarl in reply. 'I'm Alec Johnson. I own these cabins and I'm holding you responsible for the back cabin being burned down,' he shouted.

I looked at him in total surprise. 'You are holding me responsible?' I asked. 'I didn't start the fire.'

'But you were the one they were targeting. If you weren't here, my cabin wouldn't have been set on fire. Here's a bill for the replacement,' he snarled, thrusting his piece of paper towards me.

'I am sure you know the guy who set the fire is now in jail. Take that bill to him,' I suggested.

'He doesn't have any money, but you do.'

'Then take the bill to your insurance company.'

'It wasn't insured,' he said shortly.

'Not insured? More fool you.'

'Get out now! I'm evicting you!' he shouted.

'I'll get out when I'm ready. My rent was paid in advance, so I'll make the decision about when to leave,' I replied strongly.

'I'm calling the police. They'll get you out now,' he shouted.

By this time, his voice was hysterical.

'Call them,' I said quietly. They'll probably lock you up for being a public nuisance.'

'John Marshall said you would be like this,' he shouted.

He pulled a pistol from his pocket.

'So, John Marshall tells you what to do, does he?' I asked.

I looked him straight in the eye. His gaze faltered.

'Maria,' I shouted. 'Bring your pistol. We have vermin to exterminate.'

She came running, her pistol in her hand. She peered out the door around me and saw the cabin owner holding his pistol in a very shaky hand. She pointed her pistol at his heart holding it steadily and looking extremely competent.

'Drop it!' she commanded loudly and clearly.

He dropped his weapon, and I kicked it away.

'Good thing it still had the safety catch on,' she commented.

'Smart kid!' I praised.

'Get going before I call the police,' I said firmly. 'Tell John Marshall to keep his face out of my affairs or I will be tempted to kick it in.'

The cabin owner stumbled away, muttering and cursing.

'Grab a plastic bag for his pistol,' I said. 'We'll hand it in to the police. They like collecting evidence.'

I smiled as Maria found a clean plastic bag and carefully placed the pistol in it without touching the weapon with her fingers.

'I was just about to browse through John Marshall's phone call list,' she said.

She moved back to her laptop. 'Well, look at this,' she commented, a short time later.

I peered over her shoulder and saw a list of phone numbers and the people who owned them running down the screen.

He had been calling lots of wineries, possibly to order more wine, but also, I surmised to spread his gossip far and wide. I had a vision of him sitting like a large  spider in the centre of a wide web of intrigue and gossip and mischief.

*He likes to be in control*, I thought.

'Can you see any calls with the owner of the cabins,' I asked.

'What is his name?' she asked.

'Alec Johnson,' I answered.

'Yes, there are several calls between them, one this morning.

'That would be the one suggesting he gets rid of us,' I guessed. 'He probably thinks I'll return to Adelaide. His bad luck. I'll call Emilio and tell him he has two house guests. Can you see any calls from him to Dirk Thomas?' I asked.

She scanned the list. 'Quite a few,' she answered.

'Can you see one at 1.17 this afternoon?'

'Yes. Why?'

'That's when we left his restaurant. I'm sure he was directing Dirk Thomas to chase us and run us off the road. We must remember to tell the Sergeant about that call,' I said.

'Sean, do you think it is time we got out of this place?' Maria asked.

The question hung between us for a few moments.

'I guess it is time,' I agreed.

I lifted my phone and called Emilio, but he was on his way to Stanthorpe with the wine, so I left a message. I knew he wouldn't mind having us back at Top of the Range.

We packed our things and set off. I had Maria's small case and laptop on the fuel tank in front of me. Maria squeezed herself and some other bits and pieces in a pillowcase onto the pillion seat.

Mia was surprised to see us with baggage in hand, but quickly found a bedroom for us.

'You will want to share?' she asked.

'Yes, please,' Maria replied.

Mia liked buzzing around doing things for her guests. We unpacked while she set a table with some lunch for us. She was a hostess supremo, I complimented. She smiled.

After lunch Maria set up her laptop again while I borrowed a car and went back for my big case and the rest of the food stuffs.

Bella was beginning to post information from some of her Super Sleuth groups. It was a half day holiday for senior students and some of them were already investigating the rental caravans, storage sheds and containers that were parked around Stanthorpe. Nothing positive had yet been found.

The Red Panthers group had followed a man who was carrying food and drink and heading towards one of the storage containers. They thought he might be taking food to a prisoner, but they were disappointed when they saw him sit under a shady bush to have a quiet lunch.

The Green-Eyed Monster group reported that John Marshall had visited the gym, not to get exercise, but to collect a parcel from someone seated in the waiting room. They reported the parcel was small and heavy. It could have been a gun. Maria checked the time and concluded it was possibly the gun the cabin owner had waved around.

I called the police sergeant to report both the incident with the cabin owner and John Marshall's trip to the gym earlier that morning.

'It is time we brought Marshall in for some questioning,' he said.

'Hold off a little,' I suggested. 'We'll bring in that gun for your fingerprint expert to check. We'll also bring in some evidence of interesting phone calls Marshall has taken and made.'

'OK,' he said, 'but don't leave it too long.'

'In the meantime, I'll send the boys out to bring in the cabin owner. He certainly has a few questions to answer,' the sergeant said.

'Good idea,' I complimented.

'By the way,' said the Sergeant, 'I like the way the Super Sleuths are turning up useful information. That was a smart move. Never heard of it being done before. We might be able to use them for other investigations. I think you've started something positive,' he said.

# Chapter Seventeen

Maria went back to her laptop. She brought up the new phone checking software and chose John Marshall's number again. She browsed the calls made to him and those from him.

As Maria's eyes roamed down the lengthy list of Marshall's calls, she reported to me some of the interesting people he called or had calls from. We could guess many of those calls related to his compulsion to gather and spread local information about people and events in the district. But nothing stood out as important to us. Suddenly she sat up straight in her chair.

'Come and look at this,' she called to me. Quick!'

I raced over and stood behind her, staring down at the screen.

'Look at this bunch of calls to and from the Toowoomba Mental Hospital, she said loudly as if I was still at the other side of the room. 'Why would John Marshall be talking with the Toowoomba Mental Home?'

'That could be where Antonio is!' we said together.

'But he might have another reason for making those calls,' suggested Maria.

I looked at her. 'Like what?' I asked.

'Perhaps he has a relative there or something. Let me check.'

I couldn't fault her looking at all the options. *That's what makes her a good researcher*, I thought.

Her fingers raced across the keyboard. Soon a list of the names of the patients at that hospital rolled down the screen. Not one had the surname, Marshall.

'Can we find who he has been talking with?' I asked.

She called up another part of her magic software to search the hospital's phone call list. After a few moments she turned to me and said, 'All those calls have been with the administrator. None of them have been with a patient so we can be reasonably sure he doesn't have a relative in that hospital.'

'So, we can assume,' I said slowly, 'that it is possible he has lodged Antonio there.'

'It is possible,' Maria agreed.

Maria jumped up into my arms and we danced and laughed loudly like dervishes.

Mia ran into the room. 'What is going on?' she said loudly. 'It sounds like the sky is falling in.'

'We think we know where Antonio might be!' we shouted together.

We each reached out an arm and dragged her into our crazy dance. Tears ran down her face as she danced and jumped, laughed, and cried.

Emilio ran into the room. 'Do we have another firebomb?' he shouted.

'No,' we shouted together. 'We think we know where Antonio might be.'

He joined us in our crazy leaping, dancing, laughing, crying frenzy.

Eventually we ran out of steam and slowed down to a family hug.

'Tell me,' Emilio asked when we had quietened down. 'Where do you think our boy could be?'

'Toowoomba Mental Hospital,' answered Maria.

"Why a mental hospital?' asked Mia.

I thought for a minute. 'Because that is where they could keep him sedated,' I answered.

Then I had another thought. 'The fact that there have been several calls in the last few days could mean that Marshall intends to move him. We need to act quickly.'

I grabbed my phone and called the police sergeant.

As soon as the sergeant answered I said, 'We think we know where Antonio might be. It's possible he could be in the Toowoomba Mental Hospital. We think Marshall could be getting ready to move him because he thinks we are getting too close.'

'I won't ask how you know all this, but I assume you have evidence. What are you suggesting?' he asked.

'Two things, Sergeant,' I began.

'Call me Bill,' he interrupted. 'I think we are good enough friends for that now.'

'Okay, Bill. Firstly, I suggest you bring in Marshall for questioning as quickly as you can. That will give us time to grab Antonio, if he is in that hospital, before Marshall gets to him and moves him somewhere else.'

'Okay, That's easy. I'll get the troops onto that straight away. Anything else?'

'Could you ask a couple of detectives from Toowoomba to go to the Mental Hospital and check if Antonio is there. If they find him, he will probably be drugged so they may have to commandeer an ambulance to get him back here to Top of the Range Winery. If he is there, they should not leave his side until he is loaded into the ambulance.'

'I'll need a photo. Can you organise that? Evidence?' he enquired.

'I'll text a photo immediately. We'll be there shortly,' I answered. 'I'll just get Maria to print out a report of Marshall's phone calls.'

'List of his phone calls? I don't think I even want to know where they came from. But we do need the evidence,' he rationalised. He closed the call.

Maria took her laptop into Jane's office and connected it to a printer. She set to work printing out a comprehensive list of calls in and out of Marshall's phone.

I asked Mia for a photo of Antonio. I photographed it with my phone then sent it by text to the sergeant. I then collected the cabin owner's gun and stored that safely in one of the bike's panier bags. Maria came out to the bike with a satchel holding her printouts. We donned our leather jackets and helmets and off we rode to the Stanthorpe Police Station.

Once there, we were ushered into Bill's office. He greeted us and took possession of the reports and the gun.

'We have the cabin owner in one room and Marshall in the other. I'll go from one to the other checking their stories about the gun. I'll have fun asking Marshall about some of these phone calls,' he commented after he had run his eye down the latest report.

'Good luck,' I said as he walked to the door.

He turned. 'By the way, your guess was right. The detectives found Antonio in the hospital. He is still heavily drugged, so they are now trying to organise an ambulance. They have had fun asking awkward questions of the chief administrator about his dealings with Marshall. He will be facing charges over his part in this deception.'

The sergeant left the room with a wide smile on his face.

'I'm guessing he likes to catch criminals,' I commented to Maria.

'Don't know how you got that idea,' she said with a wide smile. 'I must admit I enjoy finding the evidence to put them away.'

'Now we have to concentrate on who tried to take our heads off,' I said.

I quickly phoned Emilio with the good news and told him to expect the ambulance carrying his son soon. He sobbed his thanks and called to Mia. I hung up. I would let them celebrate together.

'Come and look at this with me,' said Maria as she took another report from her satchel. 'I made two copies of Marshall's phone calls. We might find the other murderer on this list.

We sat together going through Marshall's phone calls. Maria grabbed a pen so we could mark anyone who seemed likely.

As we worked, the Sergeant came back into his office with a big grin on his face.

'Glad I came to work today,' he said. 'Thank you for providing me with something interesting to do instead of the usual boring routine. The cabin owner has cracked. He is spilling everything. He admitted telling Marshall that Emilio booked Sean's cabin. He also told us that Marshall provided him with the gun to threaten Sean and told him what to say. Marshall is a tougher nut to crack but is beginning to admit to some of the stuff we already know from other sources. He keeps asking for a lawyer, but he will have to wait.'

He turned to Maria. 'I am indebted to you for that list of Marshall's phone calls. We will have to get an official list from the phone company for the court, but your list is brilliant. I don't suppose you would like to work for me fulltime?'

She smiled but shook her head. 'I already have a fulltime job with Sean. The pay is woeful, but the side benefits are great. With you I wouldn't have the fun of being nearly murdered two or three times a week.'

We all laughed.

'Well, thank you both. I've enjoyed the last week or so. It's a treat to work with professionals.'

'It hasn't ended,' I added. 'We still have to find our fencing wire murderer.'

'We will continue investigating this, but I encourage you to keep digging into this matter too,' said Bill. 'Just a moment,' he said as a phone call was diverted to his desk.

He picked up the receiver and took the call, 'Great,' he said to the caller. 'Thank you for your efforts.'

He replaced the phone on its cradle and turned to us with a huge grin on his face. 'The detectives have released Antonio from the hospital and have seen him loaded into an ambulance for his journey home. They have also charged the hospital administrator for his part in this deception. He has confirmed Marshall paid him $10,000 to keep the boy drugged. Now we have enough to put him in jail too,' he said, his face breaking into a wide smile.

We thanked him and left the station.

# Chapter Eighteen

When we returned to the winery, the ambulance staff were just unloading Antonio. We took a close look and could tell he was still drugged, just beginning to try to open his eyes, and attempting to lift his head off the pillow. Mia ran out and hugged her son. Tears of joy cascaded down her face. This was the best moment of her life.

We followed as the ambos began wheeling their trolley into the building. Lucia ran out and joined Mia as she walked alongside the trolley holding onto Antonio's arm. They were both still laughing and crying as they left the trolley and grabbed a couch to drag into the main dining room.

I raced over to give them a hand. Antonio was lifted from the ambulance trolley onto the couch. Mia picked up a blanket and tucked it around him then sank down beside him taking his hand.

Emilio rushed in. He ran to the couch and wrapped his arms around his son. We could see tears beginning to run down his face. He looked up at Maria and I and whispered a grateful thanks. Maria grabbed a tissue from her handbag and moved to wipe the tears from his face. He grabbed her hand and covered it with kisses.

I looked around the room and saw several other people standing quietly and wiping tears from their eyes, while

Antonio was settled. I was surprised to see Bella and her mother. I prodded Maria and quietly indicated where she should look.

She smiled when she saw Bella and gave a little wave.

Mia noticed where Maria was looking. She waved to Bella and motioned for her to come over to her. Bella gave a little jump of surprise and excitement and immediately stepped across the room. Mia whispered to her that she should sit on the couch to be near Antonio when his eyes began to focus.

Bella sank down on the couch next to Mia who had a firm grip of her son's arm. Antonio's mother put her other arm around Bella, a clear sign of her acceptance of the young girl as a suitable companion for her son.

I didn't know how Bella's mother came to be here, but I guessed that Mia and Lucia had something to do with it. She watched the signs of acceptance by the boy's mother with a small smile.

Lucia bent down and whispered to Mia who nodded but stayed on the couch holding her son's hand firmly. Lucia walked to the kitchen and soon returned with trays of snacky foods. Mia's other sister-in-law, Angelina, followed them with a tray of drinks. They moved around the room offering refreshments to everyone.

A little later, Antonio opened his eyes with some comprehension. He reached to touch his mother and she bent to kiss him and hold him in a firm hug. Then he saw Bella sitting near, tears running down her face. He tried to reach her, so Mia stood to let Bella move closer. She took

Bella's place at the end of the couch, still within reach of her son. Antonio used one hand to lift the other and reached across to take Bella's hand. Bella copied Emilio and covered his hand with kisses.

I looked around the room. I don't think there was a dry eye anywhere. Everyone was overwhelmed by the pathos, and beauty of this homecoming of the prodigal son.

Much later, Antonio recovered enough from his weeklong drug-induced state to sit up. He looked at Bella.

'Why did you write me a note to bring lots of money and come to meet you?' he asked.

She gulped before being able to speak. 'That wasn't me.' She burst into tears. 'M…m… my father wrote that. I didn't know about it until later. He has done many bad things and is now with the police.'

'Police?' questioned Antonio. 'What else has he done?'

'Grabbed you for starters,' she said, 'and hid you in the Toowoomba Mental Hospital where they have kept you drugged.'

Antonio grappled with these thoughts. His mind was still foggy. 'I think I remember two men grabbing me and putting me to sleep with something held to my nose.'

I leaned over the back of the couch.

'That would have been chloroform,' I said. 'My name is Sean and I have been one of the people looking for you. Can you remember anything about the two men who grabbed you?'

He struggled to marshal his thoughts. 'I only remember smells. One smelled of food and wine, and the other smelled of something else. I don't know what.'

Maria moved alongside me and leaned over the back of the couch alongside me. 'Hi, Antonio. My name is Maria. I have been helping Sean to look for you. The man smelling of food and wine would be Bella's father. When you feel better, we need you to help us find the other man. He tried to kill Sean and I and we want him in jail too.'

Antonio looked surprised, then his eyes closed for a moment. 'Can you help me with smells?'

'I'm sure we can,' she answered. 'Rest now. We will talk again in the morning.'

Antonio's eyes closed and his head dropped back to the pillow. The hand that Bella was holding went limp.

'Come,' called Mia to everyone. 'Let us leave him sleeping. We will go into the next room for a meal.'

She began shooing people out the door, waving her hands and arms like flags. When they walked into the next room, Lucia and Angelina ushered the people to seats around two large tables. Soon plates covered with delicious food and glasses of wine began to appear on the tables.

Maria and I waited until last. We watched Bella walk over to her mother and take her hand. She brought her over to where we were standing.

'This is Maria, and this is Sean. They are the marvellous people who helped me set up the Super

Sleuths so we could search for Antonio in an ordered way,' she explained.

She smiled nervously but greeted us warmly and reached out her hand.

As we shook hands, Maria said, 'I'm pleased to meet you. You have a very intelligent and capable daughter and we have been delighted to work with her to find Antonio.'

'Your daughter,' I added, 'is an exceptionally good organiser. All her school friends hold her in high regard. You should be enormously proud of her.'

'I believe your name is Betty,' said Maria. 'May we call you that.'

'Oh, of course,' she answered quickly. 'How rude of me. I am very annoyed that my husband has caused so much grief. How can you ever forgive me for not knowing my husband was involved in this crime and not stopping him?'

'We have nothing to forgive you for. You didn't know what he was up to,' I said. 'Let's follow the others and leave Antonio to sleep off his drugged state.'

* * *

The next morning, Antonio was in a much more wakeful state. He joined us for breakfast and asked to be introduced to us.

I guessed he would have remembered very little of what had transpired the last evening.

His mother hovered over him, making sure he got everything he liked for breakfast.

After the introductions and some breakfast, Maria and I took Antonio to sit with us at our outside table under the huge fig tree.

Maria began. 'Last night you said that the two men who grabbed you had different smells. Most people emanate a scent or aroma picked up as they work.'

I took over. 'Bakers will carry scents of flour and buns and bread, or whatever they are baking. When you are winemaking, you will carry odours of grapes and wine and the chemicals you use in that process. A saddle maker will carry scents of leather, and so on. To help you remember that second person, we will introduce you to a number of different objects to see if we can find something to trigger your memory. Don't panic. It could take some time.'

He looked at us thoughtfully. 'Are you two professional investigators?'

'Yes,' said Maria. 'You could call us that. Our purpose is to help innocent people and make sure bad guys are dealt with by the police.'

'Last night I think Bella said her father was with the police. I've forgotten what she told me. What has he done?' asked Antonio.

'What hasn't he done is more the question,' I answered. 'He changed Bella's Messenger note to you to entice you to bring money, supposedly for her. He arranged to grab you and place you in the Mental Hospital where they were instructed to keep you under sedation. We are still chasing the man who helped him because we believe he tried to kill us at Bella's father's suggestion. There is more, but that is enough to be going on with.'

'Wow!' Antonio said. 'What did he do with the money I had with me?'

'The police sergeant told us it was used to bribe the Chief Administrator at the hospital,' I replied.

Antonio lapsed into silence. This was too much for him to assimilate in his still weakened state.

'Let's get positive,' added Maria. 'We'll introduce you to some smells to see if they trigger your memory.'

I commented thoughtfully. 'The guy used a wire tensioner to set up the wire trap for us. I'm guessing that he has had experience on a farm and may work in a farm associated industry.'

'Like poultry farming,' said Maria.

'What about milk?' asked Antonio.

'Could be fruit farming,' I suggested. 'Antonio, are you up to visiting some shops?

'Yes,' he answered. 'We must solve this mystery.'

'Good lad,' I replied. 'We'll need to borrow a vehicle.'

'We could take my car,' Antonio suggested, 'I believe Dad got it back here, but I'm not up to driving yet.'

'Good idea,' replied Maria. 'Let's go.'

# Chapter Nineteen

Our first stop was the fruit juice factory I had visited a few days earlier. We tried different fruit juices and Maria, and I held our glasses near Antonio's nose.

'Nothing happening so far,' he commented disappointedly.

We drove to the fruit and vegetable stall where we held different fruits and vegetables near his nose. Again, we drew a blank.

'Let's go to a big supermarket,' suggested Maria. 'They have both Woolworths and IGA in Stanthorpe.'

We walked into the Woolworths store and began in the fruit and veg aisles. I picked up a shopping basket, so we would appear to be normal shoppers.

Antonio sniffed and sniffed but nothing triggered a memory. Next, we tried the milk, cream and cheese section but again drew a blank.

'Let's try the meat section,' suggested Maria.

Most of the meats were in plastic packs. Antonio lifted a few of them to his nose for a sniff. One of the store attendants watched us, obviously concerned about this unusual buying behaviour.

I lifted a piece of steak where the covering had been partly opened. Antonio took a sniff and closed his eyes.

'Let me try that one again,' he asked.

 I lifted it to his nose again.

'Yes, I recognise that smell,' he said in a loud voice.

People around us stared at this strange behaviour. I threw the pack into my basket.

'Let's get out of here,' I whispered.

We headed for the counter and paid for the meat pack.

Once outside, we stood together and smiled.

'So your attacker had a meat smell,' I said. 'He must be a butcher or a meat worker. Where is the closest abattoir?'

Antonio replied, 'I think there might be one in Warwick. That's about 60 kms away.'

'Let's concentrate on local butchers first,' I suggested.

I looked at Maria. 'I think we have another job for our Super Sleuths.'

She nodded. 'Would Bella be home?' she asked.

I looked at Antonio. 'Do you know?'

'I think she will be still at school,' he answered.

Maria took out her phone. 'I'll find out.'

She typed a text message and received a response quickly. She read it and said, 'She asks us to pick her up at the school in ten minutes.'

'Tell her, okay,' I said.

Antonio smiled from ear to ear. He looked forward to spending some more time with his sweetheart.

We collected Bella and drove her home. She and Antonio sat in the back seat holding hands.

When we reached the restaurant, we waved to Bella's mother. She was busy with lunch guests, so we walked through the restaurant area quickly and followed Bella up the stairs to her bedroom.

She opened her laptop and looked at Maria.

'How many butcher shops are there in Stanthorpe?' Maria asked.

Bella's fingers flew over the keyboard. She was almost as quick as Maria, I noticed.

'There are two,' she replied.

'Can you tell us the names of those butchers?'

She tapped away for a while then waited for a response from the Internet. She printed out a report and handed it to Maria.

'I will need to go home and check this against my files,' she said. 'I didn't bring my printed report with me. Can we go now?' she asked me.

'We certainly can. I assume you want to check those names against Bella's father's phone list.'

'Good boy,' she teased. 'You're getting quicker.'

I poked my tongue out at her in jest.

'Can I come too?' asked Bella.

Maria nodded. 'Bring your laptop. We may have more tasks for the Super Sleuths.'

Bella smiled and closed her laptop, tucking it under her arm.

Antonio had been watching all this, a confused look on his face.

Bella put her free arm through his. 'It will all become clear to you very soon,' she said, a wide smile on her face.

As we passed through the restaurant, she ran to her mother for a quick cuddle. 'More sleuthing to do,' she said.

'Please be careful,' said her mother.

As soon as we reached the winery, Maria ran to find her laptop. She opened the list of Marshall's phone calls and compared it with the list of names Bella had printed.

'I think we have it,' she cried a few moments later. 'Our villain could be Gary Fielding. I'll check his phone calls.'

She searched for his phone number then opened it up to check his calls. 'Lots of calls and texts to Marshall she said. 'I'll check his texts.'

She tapped away on the keyboard until a line of texts ran down the screen.

'Here we are,' she said triumphantly. 'He texted Marshall to tell him he has set the wire trap.'

I immediately lifted my phone and dialled the local police sergeant. When the call was taken, I spoke quickly.

'Bill, it's Sean. We are reasonably sure our attempted murderer is the butcher, Gary Fielding.'

I listened to his response.

'Okay. We'll keep the Super Sleuths out of the picture until you have pulled him in for questioning. Don't forget about the fingerprints on the fencing wire tensioner.'

A loud outburst from the phone could be heard by the others in the room.

'I'm sorry, Bill. I didn't mean to tell you how to do your job. We have been his target, so we are anxious to have him put away as quickly as possible.'

I closed the call and turned to Bella. 'Let your team of Super Sleuths know who the potential murderer is but tell them to keep right away from him. Tell them the police are dealing with this one.'

'Okay,' she replied. She turned to her computer, typed my message, and sent it on its way.

Antonio watched all this in wonder. 'Do you have a secret society?' he asked Bella.

She smiled. 'Sort of,' she said. 'Some of my classmates decided they wanted to help me find you. The police sergeant came to the school and talked to them about how to operate without breaking the law, and Sean talked to them about keeping safe. They all report to me, and I report to Maria. She records everything they find. Those reports are given to the police.'

'Wow! All this to find me. I'm overwhelmed.'

'You're worth it,' she said.

He gave her a big hug.

'But it has grown beyond that. My father got other people involved in grabbing you and then attempting to murder Sean and Maria because he thought they were getting too close to the truth.'

Antonio turned and looked us. 'Were you two the ones who found where I was?'

Maria nodded.

'I will never be able to thank you enough,' he said. The words reflected a quiver in his voice. A few tears gathered in his eyes.

'Seeing you alive and close to Bella again is thanks enough,' I replied. 'Just look after that girl. She is one in a million.' Then I corrected myself. 'These two wonderful females are a special two in a million.'

Maria looked at me. "I think you have kissed the Blarney Stone.'

Bella and Antonio looked at her, not understanding the phrase.

Maria explained, 'It's an old Irish tradition. I'll explain it later.' She smiled at me.

'How can you say such an awful thing to a simple Irish lad.'

'More Blarney,' she said. 'Get away with you. We have work to do.'

'You've been studying Irish speech patterns,' I accused.

'Guilty as charged, your honour,' she said, a wide smile on her face.

Bella asked Maria for an explanation of the Irish speech patterns.

'Come with me,' I said to Antonio.' I want you to show me what you do in the winery.'

He was reluctant to leave Bella, but she waved him away.

'The girls have things to talk about. We will only get in their way.'

We wandered into the winery, and he bucked up when he got in among the wine vats and pumps and storage containers. He began talking about the things he does there and showed me some of the wines he had made. This was his world, and I could see he loved it.

He found two glasses and a large pipet to tap a barrel of his wine. He poured some into the glasses and handed one to me. We smelled and tasted, and he talked about the qualities he had tried to bring out in this wine. He was a professional and came fully alive in this world. I hoped he would take an award or two in the coming wine show.

# Chapter Twenty

The first day of the Australian Small Winemakers' Show arrived. We were up early and on our way to Stanthorpe in Emilio's new car with Emilio and Mia. Antonio had already left with his two aunties in his car. He would collect Bella on the way.

Maria and I felt a sense of trepidation. The sergeant had phoned us last evening to say they had to let the butcher go while they gathered more information. They said he was acting irrationally and saying he wasn't going down for something he hadn't done. He asked us to be careful at the wine show in case the villain tried once more to kill us. Maria was carrying a photo of him so we could recognise him if he turned up.

By the time we arrived, bands were already marching and playing their hearts out. A huge crowd was filing through the gate, paying for their tickets before spreading out to see the attractions. It was a popular event.

Emilio showed his pass, and we were shepherded through a side gate. Exhibitors had free access. Emilio waited a few moments until Antonio arrived. When his group was through the gate, we all moved into the pavilion where the team had set up the Top of the Range stand. During the day, they would hand out small tasting glasses of their wine and sell bottles. They knew it would be a busy day for them. The judges had already chosen the winners in each class and would hand out awards to the winning winemakers at the conclusion of the day.

Maria and I helped with some final setting up then left for a walk around the outside stalls to view the entertainment activities. I noticed Maria took out the photo of our would-be murderer and studied his face.

I looked at it too and saw a photo of a stout middle-aged man with a florid face. I committed the image to memory.

'Have you noticed we are being followed?' I asked a few moments later.

Maria looked around and smiled. 'I see we have some Super Sleuths as a bodyguard.'

She smiled at a couple of the young investigators close to her and they smiled back. They were obviously intent on keeping us safe.

In the distance, I saw the Mediaeval Group play-acting a fight and then conducting a victory parade.

I nodded to Maria to direct her attention towards them. 'I met one of the Mediaevalists the other day,' I said. 'She runs a winery called the Strange Birds. Her wines are made from varieties that produce less than 1% of the Australian crop.'

'Do they taste okay?' she asked.

'Yes, in their own way,' I replied.

Suddenly, there was a shout from one of the Super Sleuths as she ran towards us. She was holding a photo in her hand like the one Maria had. 'Enemy approaching from the side, fast.'

We turned and saw the butcher running towards us. He held one hand inside his coat as if he was hiding something from view.

'Quick,' I yelled. 'Run,' and I began running towards the Mediaeval Group.

Maria had no idea what was going on in my head, but she thought correctly that I would have a plan in mind and kept pace with me. I noticed the Super Sleuths keeping up as well.

We were soon among the folk in costume. They looked on in surprise as I headed for the Strange Bird lady.

'Enemy approaching. We need the protection of your weapons,' I called.

She took one look at me then looked up to see this demented, stout chap waving a meat cleaver as he approached at a run.

He was shouting, 'Let me at them! Let me at them!'

'Close up,' she shouted to her partners. 'Weapons ready to repel enemy.'

The rest of her group readied their weapons and closed up to surround us.

He suddenly came face to face with a forest of swords and pikes, all pointing at him.

'Get out of my way. I need to kill them,' he shouted as he waved his meat cleaver up and down and from side to side.

The Strange Bird lady stepped towards him with her sword at the ready, then suddenly she hit the butcher's wrist hard with the flat side of her sword. He dropped the cleaver. When he bent down to retrieve it with his other hand, four Super Sleuths fell on him and pinned him to the ground, face down.

I kicked the meat cleaver aside. 'Give me a belt someone,' I shouted.

A belt appeared. I grabbed it and dropped to bind his legs together. I pulled the belt tight and buckled it up.

'Another belt,' I yelled.

Another one appeared.

I called to the Super Sleuths, 'Drag his arms together behind his back.' They quickly managed that manoeuvre, and I belted his arms together tightly. Now he was trussed up like a Christmas Chicken.

'Thank you, Super Sleuths, your help has been fantastic. Three cheers for the Super Sleuths.' I looked up and added, 'and for the brave Strange Bird lady and her group. Hip Hip.'

'Hooray,' called all the Mediaeval players and a few other folks who had come to watch the fun.

'Again louder,' I called. 'Hip, hip.'

'Hooray!' they shouted, louder than before.

I noticed people running from every direction to find out what was happening.

Maria was already on her phone talking with the Police Sergeant. 'Bill,' she said loudly. 'We've caught our would-be murderer. He just tried to kill Sean and me again, but we had help to stop him. Do you have any police close by?'

I heard a voice, but I couldn't decipher the words.

'We are with the marvellous Mediaeval Warriors,' said Maria in answer to his question.

A reply came, then she turned to us. 'The police will be here in a moment or two.'

Officers came running up shortly after her call. They looked in surprise at the tightly belted character on the ground.

'Your prisoner, officers,' I said, pointing at the butcher, 'and that meat cleaver over there is the one he tried to kill us with.'

A policewoman pulled an evidence bag from her pocket and walked over to retrieve the meat cleaver. Others removed the belts and handed them back after replacing them with handcuffs.

The officer who had attended the two fire bombings and the crashed chase car looked at me and shook his head. "Are you ever out of trouble?'

'Not often,' I said and grinned at him.

Another uniform appeared behind the others.

'Hello, Bill,' I said. 'Got the last villain.'

'Well done, Sean. Sorry we had to let him out pending further enquiries. This attempt sorts it out nicely, I think,' he said.

The other police officers stared. They rarely saw anyone on first name terms with their boss.

'By the way, I will need any evidence you have,' he added.

'Of course. We were lucky today to be protected by these wonderful Super Sleuths,' I added. 'They were the ones who saw the butcher approaching and warned us.'

He looked around and recognised some of the faces he had seen in the classroom not so long ago. 'Well done, you,' he said to them.

They smiled widely, not expecting they would be recognised.

'We've had so much fun,' said one of the boys. 'Can I talk to you one day soon about how I can learn to become a detective?'

'Me too,' said another.

The Sergeant smiled. 'Ring and make an appointment. Say you are Super Sleuths.'

The lads smiled their thanks.

The sergeant turned to walk away.

I called, 'Bill, can I ask a question before you go?'

He turned. 'Of course, you can,' he answered. 'How can I help you?'

'Maria and I have been wondering what hold Marshall had over Shane's friend, Dirk, and the butcher. Why would they try to kill us on his say so? And over the cabin owner to make him threaten us like that?'

'Good question, Sean. I should have mentioned this to you before. During our investigation we picked up the answers to those questions.'

Maria came close to hear his explanation.

The sergeant smiled at her and continued. 'Money… it's the root of all evil. Dirk didn't try to kill you on Marshall's instruction. Marshall knew he was after you and rang him to let him know where you would be. You see, Shane also owed Dirk money and he tried to kill you so you couldn't prove Shane committed the robberies from Emilio. If Shane went to jail, he would lose the money owing to him.

'The butcher was a different story. He loves buying property but over-extended himself and Marshall bailed him out and took over the loan. He threatened to foreclose if he didn't agree to do as he asked. That would leave him without his butcher shop, which he had heavily mortgaged, and no income.

'The cabin owner was in deep debt to the bank over the cabins and they weren't insured. Marshall supplied the gun and agreed to rebuild the burnt cabin if he could make you leave. I think he was hoping he would lose it and shoot you if you didn't agree to pay.'

'Boy,' I said. 'What power that man has gathered. Glad he is now safely behind bars where he can't hurt anyone else.'

'Let's hope the court agrees with you. Only time will tell.'

We stood and watched as Maria walked over to the Strange Bird lady. 'Can I ask if we can have a swordplay workout?' she asked.

The lady looked in surprise, then smiled and said, 'Of course.'

Someone else from the group offered Maria a sword. She swung it a few times to judge weight and balance, then smiled. 'Just right,' she said, 'thanks.'

I stood there in absolute surprise. I had no idea she knew anything about sword fighting.

They sized up, then on command began the preliminary sword manoeuvres. It was obvious Maria knew exactly what she was doing.

Soon the two women were swinging, thrusting, and blocking, starting slowly but gaining speed. They were soon going hammer and tongs. A large crowd had gathered to watch and clap.

Eventually the Strange Bird lady called a stop. They both stood there breathing hard. It had been a good workout for them both. It was obvious they were equally matched.

Maria bowed to her opponent then handed her sword back to the owner with thanks.

I rescued her from the clapping crowd, and we began walking back to the stadium. She put her arm through mine.

'You are full of surprises,' I said. 'I was very proud of you.'

'I was proud of you when you knew how to truss up that objectionable butcher,' she responded.

'Well, so much for the mutual admiration society,' I said, grinning. 'How did you learn to fight with a sword?'

'Another of Uncle Marcello's requirements.'

'Good old Marcello. He has obviously been preparing you for a dangerous life. He organised lessons for you to learn to shoot and fight with a sword. I wonder what else I will find out?'

She looked at me. 'I see now he has been preparing me for a life with you.'

I looked at her carefully. Her comment took me by surprise. My mind took me on a quick assessment of my earlier partners. None of them had enjoyed the dangerous situations my investigations led me into. Now here was someone who seemed to enjoy my dangerous life.

'Do you mean that?' I asked.

She looked at me seriously, then I saw a twinkle beginning to dance in her eyes. 'You're stuck with me now.'

'What bad luck.' I replied, a wide grin forming on my face. 'Come here.'

I reached out my arms and pulled her in close for a long, slow, and passionate kiss. We were dimly aware of a crowd gathering around us, clapping and cheering.

Eventually, we broke apart. I looked around at the crowd and shouted, 'Thank you.'

'Come,' I said to her, 'We need to watch the award giving.'

We began walking towards the stadium and many people came with us. As we entered the building, we heard a woman on a microphone announcing the award winners and calling those winemakers to the podium to receive their certificates.

A little later, she announced, 'I now have a special award for Antonio Angelica for his Shiraz Durif.'

We saw Antonio step forward and climb the steps. The crowd clapped loudly. He stood proudly in the middle of the stage waving his certificate. Then he gave a deep bow to the audience. After that, he moved to the woman and obviously asked to use the microphone. She handed it over. Antonio turned to face the crowd and lifted the microphone to his lips.

'Many of you already know that I was abducted and locked in a mental hospital under sedation. I would still be there, or even dead, if it wasn't for the excellent detective work by Sean O'Connor and Maria Antonucci. Please give them a clap.'

He pointed to us, and the crowd applauded loudly.

Antonio continued, 'Another person who contributed to finding me was my girlfriend Bella Marshall and her band of Super Sleuths.'

Many in the crowd were mystified by the term Super Sleuths but clapped loudly anyway. Bella moved to the bottom of the stage steps. Antonio handed back the microphone, climbed down the steps and was grabbed and hugged and kissed by Bella. The crowd applauded again.

We moved away and Maria looked at me. 'What now?' she asked.

'Back to boring auditing,' I said.

'It will make a nice change not to be the intended victims of murderers,' she answered. She smiled at me.

My phone rang. I opened it and answered the call.

'Sean speaking,' I said.

'Are you going back to Adelaide straight away?' asked Detective Bill Masterson.

I put the phone on speaker and held it close to Maria's ear. 'Not just yet, Bill. I have some winery auditing to do first.'

Bill's voice came clearly to both of us. 'I have a strange mystery to solve. I wonder whether you would consider helping me on one more case?'

'Yes,' shouted Maria.

'Yes,' I replied.

'It could be dangerous,' he added.

'That's a double yes from both of us,' answered Maria. Her eyes sparkled with excitement.

'We can delay the auditing work for a few days. We'll see you tomorrow,' I said and closed the call.

'Just keep a pistol and a sword handy,' I said to Maria.

'What about my clever computer?' she asked, a wide smile creasing her face.

'Yes, that too,' I agreed sweeping her into my arms.

**Dr Ron Day** holds many university degrees, including a PhD, and is a published author of a series of textbooks for use in primary, secondary, tertiary schools, and colleges.

He has had more than 30 years' experience in teaching and writing. He has recently turned his love of writing to include crime novellas.

His first exciting crime novella, *Auditing Can Be Deadly* was released in 2021 and the second, *Deceit Can be Deadly* was published in 2022. This is the third book in his crime series.

Ron is available to do author talks, book signings or workshops on writing at schools, libraries or writing groups.

Contact info@morrispublishingaustralia.com
for more information or to book.

www.ingramcontent.com/pod-product-compliance
Lightning Source LLC
Chambersburg PA
CBHW041748010726
47507CB00008B/327